The Sugar Shack
By Jordan Tipper

Contents:

Chapter 1 - Page 3

Chapter 2 - Page 6

Chapter 3 - Page 9

Chapter 4 - Page 12

Chapter 5 - Page 14

Chapter 6 - Page 18

Chapter 7 - Page 23

Chapter 8 - Page 28

Chapter 9 - Page 30

Chapter 10 - Page 33

Chapter 11 - Page 35

Chapter 12 - Page 40

Chapter 13 - Page 45

Chapter 14 - Page 49

Chapter 15 - Page 53

Chapter 16 - Page 60

Chapter 17 - Page 73

Chapter 18 - Page 82

Chapter 19 - Page 85

1

"What would you like to order?" I said to the customer as she was still standing there looking at the menu. "It's not a hard choice mother!" I said as she was getting irate with me.
"George, I will take my time." My mom replied as she was holding up the line.
"You are really clogging us." I said as she looked at me angrily.
"Do you want dinner tonight?" She responded as she then pointed to the blue sweets.
"I want lots of those." She stated.
"Okay." I said as I got out my shovel and began to shovel the sweets into the bag. "And how will you be paying for these?" I asked.
"I ain't paying, I'm your mother." She said.
"Mom, you still have to pay, this isn't the first time you have been here." I continued as I passed her the sweets.
"I'll make dinner tonight." She said as she looked at me. The customer behind her was confused.
"I want free sweets as well." They chimed in.
"Mom, I need money."
"I don't care darling." She continued as she dug into the sweets.
"I want free sweets." The next customer said as she stepped up and banged on the counter.
"There are no free sweets going." I said as the customers then became angry.
"You are scamming your customers." Someone shouted as my mom then handed out her sweets.
"Here, you can have some of these." She said as the customer snatched the bag out of her hand. The sweets all fell on the floor. "What have you done?" She said as she looked at the customer. "You have made a big mistake." She continued as she then hit them with a karate chop. There was then full on chaos in my sweet store as I was getting worried for my shop. I then rang the bell above my head as everyone stopped and looked at me.
"Give us free sweets." The people were chanting as they were getting louder and louder.
"I'm sorry, but I just can't give out free sweets to everyone."
"Then make your mother pay." Someone shouted, I rolled my eyes.
"I want her to pay, she is the one not paying." I continued as everyone looked at her. There was a big roar.
"So she is stealing." Someone yelled out.
"Technically yes!" I said as my mom was still trying to beat off all the customers.
"Please don't get me involved." She said as she ducked under the tables.
"This is all your fault." I said as I jumped off the counter and down to the ground.
"Okay, okay." She said as she reached into her purse and pulled out some money. "How much do I owe you?" She asked.
"£3.50." I said as she gave me £5.
"Keep it." She said as she took the bag of sweets and then walked out of the shop.
"Sorry about that." I said to the next customer.
"Mothers." They said as we both laughed. "My mom thinks she can get everything for free here." The customer said. "I work at this fast food shop and my mother comes in everyday looking for free fries. My name is Amy." She said as she put her hand out for it to be shook.

"My name is George." I said as I smiled. "It's nice to see a new face around these parts." I continued. "I haven't seen you around here before." I said.
"Yes, I just moved and I'm looking for some sweets for my husband."
"Oh!" I said as my smile deflated.
"Yes, just some mice for the hubby." Amy said as she let go of my hand.
"Yes yes, coming up!" I said as I grabbed my shovel and put the mice into a bag.
"Here!" I said as I threw them at her.
"HEY!" She yelled as she caught it.
"Sorry, I'm just in a rush." I continued to say as I then blanked her. "Next please!" I said. She looked at me confused.
"What's the problem? Just because I have a husband." She said as she started to get all defensive.
"Yer, yer, okay love, isn't it past your bedtime." I said as the next customer came up.
"I like some bananas please." He said.
"Yes, coming right up." Amy continued to stare at me as she was getting irate.
"SIR!" She shouted as I was serving the next customer.
"Ma'am, you can see I am serving someone else." I said as I was just trying to ignore her. Amy then began to go through her sweets and started chucking them at me while I was trying to serve the customer. I turned around and looked at her while the other customers were getting angry. "Amy, go wait in the back." I said as she looked at me confused. "Just go, I'll talk to you in a minute." I said as I handed over the bananas to the customer. "Thank you." I said as he handed over the money. "One second!" I then continued as the next customer rolled up and began to ask for sweets. I then went to the back of the shop as Amy was still angry with me.
"What you have done to me, is sexual assault." She said as I then walked over and gave her a big kiss on the lips. She then dropped her bag of sweets as I pulled her up against the table as she continued to make out with me. I then crawled onto her, as all of a sudden I pushed her away. "Shit!" I said.
"What is it sexy?" Amy asked.
"I got customers to serve." I replied as Amy laughed.
"Oh okay, don't be long." She said as she was teasing me. I got off and quickly did up my clothes as I went back to serve customers.
"Sorry about that." I said as the customer was confused.
"What was all that noise?" He asked.
"Nothing." I said as I blushed.
"Okay, can I just get some skittles!" He said as I turned around and looked at the door. "Excuse me." The man said as he kept noticing that I was distracted. "Why do you keep looking over there?" He said as I smiled.
"Oh nothing." I said as I gave him the candy. The customer then gave me the money as I kept looking at the door to the office. He left as the next customer came up.
"I like some millions." She said.
"Just one second!" I said as I headed back into the office and saw Amy laying there naked on the desk.
"Come get your candy." She said as her tits were hanging out. I then jumped on the desk as we proceeded to make out once again.

"I love you." I said to Amy as she was biting my ear.
"Oh yeah." She continued to say as all of a sudden there was a knock at the door.
"GEORGE!" Someone shouted.
"Sorry, I have to get this." I said.
"It's okay." Amy replied as all of a sudden her phone began to ring.

2

"Hey babe." The person down the line said.
"Did you get the stuff?" He said.
"Oh yer, sorry there was a line and it just took hours for me to get those sweets." Amy said.
"So, where are you now?"
"I'm just in traffic." Amy lied as she was rushing to put on her clothes.
"How long will you be?" He continued to ask.
"I will be home as soon as possible." Amy said as she got off the desk and dashed out of the office still on the phone.
"My mates are picking me up at 7." He continued. "And you promised to look after the baby."
"Yes yes, but I can't do anything about the traffic." Amy said as she waved at me as I was serving sweets. I looked at her and her ass. I just smiled.
"She's so beautiful." I said to the customer as she was confused.
"What?" The customer said.
"Oh sorry, I was thinking about someone." I said as I passed the customer the sweets. "Here you go."
"Thank you." She said as she was the last customer of the day as Amy dashed out of the shop and flagged down a taxi. I then began to chase after her.
"Where are you going?" I said as I opened the door.
"I have to go home to my husband and kid." Amy said as I got a little disappointed inside.
"Oh." I said. "But didn't that mean anything?" I said as Amy was getting in the back of the taxi.
"It did, but I can't just leave my husband of many years." She said as she slammed the door closed and the taxi began to drive off.
"I love you." I bellowed as the taxi had driven off. Amy put up a heart sign as she agreed. She then wrote down her phone number on a piece of paper and chucked it at me.
"CALL ME!" She shouted. I rushed over and picked the piece of paper. I looked at the number as I shoved it into my pocket. I couldn't believe everything was moving so fast. I turned around and went back into my shop as I had turned the open sign to close. There was no one in my shop as I looked at the clock. It was getting late.
"I better head home." I said to myself as I began tidying up. Suddenly someone came through the door. "Sorry we are closed." I said as I was handling the broom.
"G!" They said as I turned around.
"AMY?" I said as I was shocked and confused. She then locked the door behind her.
"My husband can wait." She said as she came over and kissed me on the lips. "That was the best sex I have had in ages." She continued to say as she pushed me onto the counter. "Let's do it again."
"Wow, calm down baby." I said as I undid my pants and dropped the broom. We then proceeded to have sex once again. We lasted long into the night as we had a lot of passion. It was amazing. "Oh yer." I said as I ejaculated everywhere.
"I haven't seen that amount of cum in years." Amy said as her tits were jiggling up and down. It must have been hours as we fell onto the floor.
"Oh yer." I said as Amy hit her head on the counter. She then laughed. I suddenly fell asleep as I was getting tired from all the action. The hours went by as all of a sudden there was a knock at

the store door. I woke up and quickly threw on my clothes. "Oh shit." I said as I couldn't believe someone would be knocking on my store door at this time of day. I got up and walked over to the door as Amy dashed to the back room. I opened the door to find out it was the police.
"Hello." The officer said.
"How can I help, officer?"
"Yes, we just got a report of a missing person and this was the last place she was located."
"I see, officer, but no one else is here." I said as he nodded his head.
"Well you wouldn't mind having a look around then." He said as I turned around to see the blanket still on the floor.
"Yes yes, I'm not hiding anything." I said as I then kicked the blanket behind the counter. The officers came flooding in. They began searching through the shop to make sure I wasn't hiding anything illegal. "You are wasting your time, officers."
"If you have nothing to hide, then you wouldn't mind us doing this." He continued to say.
"Well just don't make a mess." I said as suddenly there was a noise from the backroom. The officers dropped what they were holding as they then dashed into the backroom to find Amy hiding under the table.
"YOU!" The officer shouted at her. She looked at him as I came and saw the chaos.
"I have never seen that girl in my life." I said as Amy was getting out from under the table. She looked at me confused.
"What are you doing back here?" The officer asked as Amy began to sweat.
"Nothing." She said as she began to laugh.
"Why are you laughing?" The officer questioned.
"Nothing sir." She said as she got up and got placed in handcuffs.
"Do you know how much resources you have wasted?" The officer announced.
"I never said I was lost."
"Well, try telling that to your husband."
"I'm sorry officer." Amy said as you could see the sorry in her eyes. I was still being asked questions.
"How did she get in?" I was asked.
"I don't know." I lied as Amy was looking more and more angry at me.
"So you are saying you don't know how she got in, so she broke in?" The officer asked.
"Yes, I always lock my doors." I said.
"SARGE!" One of the officers shouted as they came in with a blanket. "What is this?" They asked.
"It's a blanket." I said.
"But why is it in your store?"
"I sleep here." I said. The officer nodded.
"So you're telling me you own this big store and you sleep inside the store."
"Yes, I do it to save money."
"Interesting!" The officer said as he bagged the blanket. "Do you mind if we take this down the station?"
"Sure." I said as I had nothing to hide. Amy was being escorted away in handcuffs. She looked at me.

"Don't I mean anything to you?" She said. I didn't say anything as I didn't want to get myself in trouble. The officer was still looking at me.
"Do you mind coming down the station, so we can add more to this statement?" He asked.
"I haven't done anything."
"I understand that, but we need to know how this woman got into your store if you had locked up."
"Oh yes." I said, nodding my head as the officer passed me his card.
"Give me a call tomorrow and we can arrange a time for you to go down the station and tell us everything." I took the card and placed it in my pocket.
"Yes yes." I said as all the officers left the store. I began cleaning up as the moon was going down. "I better get some sleep before I open up tomorrow." I said to myself as all of a sudden a phone began to ring. I went into the back as I had noticed that Amy had dropped her phone.
"Shit!" I said as I picked it up and answered it.
"AMY?" The voice said.
"Hello, who is this?" I asked.
"This is Terry." The voice said. "Who is this?" He replied. I began to sweat as I didn't want to reveal my name as he could figure out me and Amy were having an affair.
"My name?" I said. "My name is Roy."
"Okay Roy." He said. "Where did you get this phone?" He asked.
"Well I just found it on the floor on the street." I said, lying to him.
"Oh okay." Terry said. "Can you return it to this address?" He said as he gave out his address. I took a big breath.
"I have to see sir, I have a very busy day ahead." I replied.
"It will just take two minutes." Terry continued as I was really struggling with what I should do next.
"I have to go." I said as I pretended to fake someone knocking on the door. I then closed the phone as I then threw it against the wall. It broke into a hundred pieces. "Fucking cunt." I said under my breath as I shielded my eyes. I then looked at the mess as I grabbed the broom and began to clean up. "I shouldn't have done that!" I continued to say as the light was getting brighter and brighter. I put all the pieces I could find and placed them into the bin as I needed to get some sleep. I went into the back as I grabbed a cup of water. "Oh yeah, that is the stuff." I said as I drank the refreshing water. I then looked at the clock. "Oh god, I have to get up in 2 hours." I said as I dropped the cup of water, spilling it all over the floor. "I'll pick that up in the morning." I said as I closed the door. I jumped onto the floor as I really needed to get some sleep. I placed my head against the pillow that was still on the floor. I closed my eyes as I needed to get some sleep.

3

I fell asleep after 10 minutes of looking at the ceiling. The moon then went down as the sun came up. I then woke up as I turned over and saw the clock. "Oh god! Is it really 8am?" I questioned as I stretched my arms and got up. I then picked up the pillow and threw it into the back room as it was still wet from me spilling the water everywhere. "I'll sort that out later." I said as I was really low on energy. Someone then knocked on the door.
"Are you opening today?" They said as I was pulling up my pants. I turned around embarrassed.
"Yes yes, just one second." I said as I wiped my face and came over to the front door. "Sorry about that." I said as I opened the door.
"It's okay, I just need to get some sweets before I go take the kids to school."
"Oh okay." I said as they came in to see the mess all over the floor.
"What's been going on?" He asked.
"Nothing." I said as I rushed around the back of the counter and began to open up the sweets.
"What would you like?" I asked as I pulled up my pants.
"Just some of those." He said as he pointed to the mixed coloured one with nuts in.
"Oh, great choice!" I said as I got out the shovel and began to get them out. I put them all in the bag as he got out his credit card.
How much do I owe you?" He said.
"Oh just £3." I said as he gave me the money.
"Thank you." He said as he looked into the bag and noticed something strange in it. "What is this?" He asked as I went over and looked at it.
"The sweets you asked for?" I replied. He then looked at it again.
"These?" He said as he pulled out a set of keys. "I don't wanna be biting on metal." He jokingly said as he passed me the keys.
"Oh I'm sorry, I didn't see that." I said that as he looked at me strangely.
"Are you okay?" He asked as I put the keys in my pocket.
"You can have the sweets for free." I said as I handed back his money.
"You didn't answer me." He said as I suddenly fell to the floor. He looked at me in confusion as I hit my head on the way down. "Are you okay?" He said as I was out for the count. He rushed over to grab the phone as his sweets spilled everywhere. He then called the police and medics as he then went back to my office. He then took the keys from my desk as he then locked up the shop. I slowly managed to get up as my head was hurting from hitting the counter.
"Oh goodness." I said as I saw all the blood dripping onto the floor. I was holding my head as I was feeling dizzy. I tried to walk to the counter but I was really struggling. "HELP!" I shouted as it was getting hot in here. There was no reply as there was more and more blood coming out of my head. 10 minutes must have passed as all of a sudden there was a loud bang at the door.
"HELLO!" They shouted as I was still laying on the floor as blood was pouring out. They looked through the windows and banged on it alot. "SIR!" They shouted as I was still laying on the ground. They then kicked the door in as they rushed over and assisted me. "Sir, it's going to be okay." The medic said as they began to wrap my head up in bandages. I wasn't really focusing on what they were saying as the other medic was cleaning up the blood.
"But what about the shop?" I said slowly as I was trying to communicate with the medics.

"Sir, it would be better if you were quiet." The medic said as he placed a head brace around my neck.
"I can't." I said as I then began to shake.
"We need to get this person right to the hospital, Harold." The medic said as they began to lift me up and onto the stretcher.
"Totally." Harold replied as they were rushing me to the ambulance. I was placed on the stretcher and the ambulance began to drive off. I was still unsure what was going on. As suddenly my mobile phone began to ring. The medic grabbed it. "Hello, this is Harold from the hospital, your friend has been in a serious incident and he is being taken to hospital."
"Oh my goodness." The voice said down the line.
"Yes, sorry, I have to go." Harold said as he placed the phone down and continued to work on my head. 20 minutes went by as we were making it to the hospital, I slowly began to wake up as the medics were still force feeding me.
"Hello?" I said, all confused.
"Sir, you have been attacked." Harold said as he passed me the phone. "Someone called Amy tried calling earlier, I explained you are on the way to the hospital." I looked at him.
"No, no." I said. "You shouldn't have done that!" I said as I looked embarrassed. Harold looked at me confused.
"Why?" He said.
"We were having an affair and now she is going to come to the hospital. Her husband is going to be mad at me." I said I began to panic. Harold then took the oxygen mask off my face.
"Sorry." He said as I looked at his badge.
"Are you sure you are a real medic?" I said as he began to sweat.
"Umm...yes." He said as he pointed at his badge.
"But that is a fake." I said as I got up from the stretcher and looked at him eye to eye. "Don't I know you." I questioned.
"Sir, I suggest you go back to sleep." He said, trying to dodge the questions.
"I know you from school." I said as he looked embarrassed. "You used to bully me." I then announced as he then put the oxygen mask back onto me.
"Go back to sleep." Harold said as he was holding the mask over me, choking me.
"Stop!" I said under the mask as I tried to wrestle it off him. The ambulance then pulled up to the hospital as we came to a slow stop. The other medic came out and opened up the doors.
"Oh! You are doing better." She said. "That is good." She continued as Harold was just looking there confused. "Harold, come on."
"Sorry sorry." Harold said as I was still laying under the oxygen mask being taken out on the stretcher. The blood had stopped going to my brain.
"HAROLD!" The other medic shouted as he had taken his eye off the ball. "Come on!" She yelled as Harold then began to cry. "Oh, come on!" She said as she was handling the stretcher all by herself. Harold then jumped out of the ambulance and walked out. She then took control of the stretcher as other medics came out to help me as Harold ran around the corner. I was being escorted in as I was feeling better than before but still had to be looked over by the medics. "You are going to be okay." The medic said. I was getting better but had to go in for an emergency operation.

"Sir, we need to stitch your head up." The doctor said as I was still under the oxygen mask.
"What happened to Harold?" One of the other doctors asked.
"He just needed some fresh air." The medic replied as I then got up and looked around the room. "She isn't here is she?" I said.
"Who?" The doctor asked.
"The medic accidentally called my mistress and I don't want her here." I said as they were still working on my skull.
"No, no one has arrived just yet." The doctor said.
"Oh good." I replied as they put something in me.
"This is just something to make you sleepy." The doctor announced.
"Okay." I said as I suddenly got a headache. "I love you." I said to the doctor as he looked at me strangely. I then went to sleep as the doctors then rolled me into the theater room.

4

Meanwhile Amy was making her way to the hospital. "I hope he is okay." She said to herself as she was sitting on the bus. The lady next to her looked at her.
"What's up?" She asked.
"Nothing." Amy replied as she began to get tearful.
"You can talk to me." The old lady said.
"No no, it's fine." Amy repeated as the old lady placed her hand on Amy.
"It's okay." She said as Amy looked at her.
"Okay." She replied. "I've been having an affair." Amy suddenly blurted out loudly as everyone on the bus turned around and looked at her.
"Well, that seems to be your problem." The old lady said as she turned around.
"No. Please!" Amy begged as the old lady had turned off. "It wasn't a mistake, I fell in love with him but I still love my husband." Amy explained.
"I suggest you get locked up for being crazy in the head." The old lady said as she was starting to ignore Amy.
"Oh come on, like you have never thought about cheating on your husband." Amy said as she came up close and personal with the old lady. The lady turned around.
"Ma'am, please give me space." Amy then slapped the old lady as she fell to the ground.
Everyone turned around and looked at Amy standing over the old lady, who was laying on the floor of the bus.
"What have you done?" Someone shouted as everyone was rushing over to assist the old lady.
"You are going to be in a lot of trouble." A man said as he grabbed Amy and put her arms around her back.
"What are you doing?" She asked as the man grabbed her closer.
"You are under arrest." He said as he pulled out his undercover badge.
"But it was an accident." Amy explained as she was embarrassed. All of a sudden her phone began to ring. "I really need to get this." Amy said as the man opened up the phone and gave it to her.
"Where are you?" Terry said down the line.
"I told you, I need to go see my friend in the hospital." Amy said as everyone on the bus was making a lot of noise.
"Why is everyone booing you?" Terry asked down the line.
"They aren't booing me, they are booing the bus driver as we have been stuck in traffic for over 20 minutes." Amy said as she was twisting the truth. The man then took the phone off her.
"Sir, your wife has been lying, she is under arrest for assaulting someone." Terry was shocked.
"No, you can't be telling the truth." He shouted down the line. "My wife is honest and trustworthy." He said to the officer. Amy then began to laugh.
"What's so funny?" The officer said as Amy was smirking. Amy then grabbed the phone and put it down.
"You don't need to know." She said as the bus stopped.
"Okay, everyone off." The bus driver said as the old lady was still on the floor. Blood was still coming out from her head.

"We need to get her some medical aid." Someone said on the bus as everyone was looking at Amy.
"Look, it was an accident." Amy said as she was being pulled off the bus. Everyone was booing as Amy was being taken off the bus. "Please don't arrest me." Amy said to the officer.
"I'm sorry." The officer said as he then pulled out his radio and radioed for backup. Amy looked at him as she then began to sweat.
"I can't go to prison." Amy said.
"You have to do the time.!" The officer replied as all of a sudden there was a police car behind the bus.
"PLEASE!" Amy shouted as the officer got out of the car and then walked over to her.
"Take her down the station Phil." The officer holding Amy said.
"No, please!" Amy said as she dropped to her knees.

5

Meanwhile the medics were rushing to the scene as they were trying to save the old lady. Amy was placed in the back of the police car as she was then escorted down the station. I was out of the theater as I was recovering from the operation. I was laying in my hospital bed as I slowly woke up. The medic was looking after me. "Take it easy." The medic said as she was injecting something into my arm.
"Ow!" I said as I woke up. "How long was I out?" I asked as the medic was looking at my eyes.
"Just a few hours." The medic said.
"Is she here?" I then asked.
"Who?" The medic replied.
"Amy?"
"No no, no one has turned up."
"Oh!" I replied as I was still looking around the medical room. "How long will I be here for?" I asked.
"As soon as you are ready to leave." The medic said as she was doing a once over on me. "I will get the doctor in just to double check a few things." The medic said as I took a sip of water. Suddenly there was a knock at the door. "Come in!" The medic said as I put down my cup.
"George." The man said. I looked at him unsure of who he was.
"Yes?" The medic said.
"Excuse me miss, that isn't any of your business." He said as the medic was then getting nervous.
"Okay, I'll give you a second alone." She said as she left the room.
"George!" The man said again.
"Who are you?" I asked. "I don't know you." I said as I sat up.
"You are right." The man said as he pulled out a folder from his pockets out of his trenchcoat. He placed it on the counter as I was confused as fuck.
"What is this?" I said.
"I saw what you did." The man said as he placed images on the table.
"I haven't done anything." I said as I began to defend myself.
"This is you, right?" The man said as he pointed to the pictures on the table. I didn't answer as I began to sweat. "This is you and a married woman." The man said.
"Can't you just leave me alone?" I said to him.
"No!" The man said. I looked him in the eyes.
"So what do you want?" I asked him as he was playing with his beard.
"I want you to come clean to the woman's husband."
"Or what?" I replied as I took another sip of water.
"I will tell them myself."
"I don't even know you dude, why would I listen to you." I said as he pulled out another piece of paper.
"You remember this George?" He said as he passed it over to me. I looked at it.
"I haven't seen this in years." I said as he then laughed. "Where did you get this from?" I asked as I began to try to rip it up.

"So, you believe me now?" The man said as he continued to chuckle. "And you can't rip that up." He said.
"At least tell me your name." I said to him,
"My name is Billy." The man said.
"Okay Billy, so what's stopping me from getting the police involved." I said as I held onto the piece of paper.
"You go to the police, you will regret it." Billy said as all of a sudden the medic came back and knocked on the door. She slowly opened it as Billy rushed to pick up all the pieces of paper.
"May I come back in?" She asked.
"Yes!" Billy said as he put all his paper into the folder and walked away.
"So what was that about?" The medic questioned me. I looked at her and then back at the piece of paper I was holding.
"That's none of your business." I said to her.
"Oh sorry." She said as you could hear the sorry in her voice. She then proceeded to inject something into me. "This will get your blood levels up." She continued as I was holding onto the bed.
"Ow!" I said as it really hurt. Meanwhile Billy was walking down the hallways of the hospital as all of a sudden he bumped into a doctor.
"Hey, why don't you mind where you are going?" Billy said to the doctor as he spilled his coffee on himself.
"Why don't you mind where you are going?" The doctor replied as Billy had dropped his folder. The papers were soaked with coffee.
"You have ruined everything!" Billy said as he grabbed the doctor and shoved him into the nearest toilet.
"What are you doing?" The doctor said as he was still recovering from dropping his coffee. Billy then shoved the doctor's head down the toilet as he gave him a swirly.
"Don't you ever backchat me ever again!" Billy said as the doctor was screaming.
"Why must you do this?" The doctor said as his face was in the toilet bowl. All the germs flew into his mouth.
"Fuck you." Billy said as he kicked the doctor then walked out of the door and out of the room. Billy then picked up his folder that was covered in coffee as he then began to wipe it down as everyone else was looking at him. "What?" Billy said angrily as he looked everyone in the eyes. He then walked off as it was really awkward.
"Sir, we have operations to deal with."
"So what!" He said to another doctor as he flipped the table over and made a mess.
"Jan get the police on the line." The doctor said as Jan rushed to the phone and called for the police. The hospital security came rushing in as they grabbed Billy and held him up against the wall.
"I suggest you don't do that." Billy said as he pulled something out his pocket. It was a gun. He pointed it at the doctors.
"Sir, you are not well."
"Don't do anything or I will shoot." Billy said as he suddenly got angry with the medical staff. The doctors were panicking as one of them suddenly pulled the fire alarm.
"We need to get everyone out!" One of the doctors said as Billy was rattering the gun.

"Shut up!" He repeated as all of a sudden he pulled the trigger and a bullet fired. It went right into a doctor's chest and he fell to the floor.
"Sir, please!" One of the other doctors said as all of a sudden Billy was then rugby tackled by the security. He was still wrestling with the gun as a second bullet then went off. It went right through the ceiling of the hospital as Billy was biting the guards. The police then arrived with tasers. They shocked him as he dropped the gun onto the floor.
"Sir, you are under arrest for obvious reasons." Billy was shocked as he didn't know what was really happening.
"I didn't do anything." He stated as he suddenly curled up into a ball and started to cry.
"Take him away, boys." The officer said as the other officers took Billy down the hallway and down into the police car. Everyone was rushing to assist the doctor that was shot.
"Daniel, it's going to be okay." One of the nurses said as they took off his shirt and started covering the blood that was pouring out of Daniel's chest.
"We need a ten CC stat." Someone else said as Billy was being led away in handcuffs.
"I didn't do anything." He continued to say. All of a sudden something dropped out of his coat pocket.
"What's this?" The officer said as he picked it up and looked through it, he saw a ton of pictures of people. "Who are all these people?" The officer asked. Billy didn't say anything as he then went red. "Sir, are you stalking people?" The officer said.
"No no, it's not what you think." Billy shouted out as he was just about to be put into the police car. The officers bagged up the folder as I was still trying to figure out what happened from my hospital bed.
"How did he get all of that?" I said to myself as I was looking at everyone who was coming in and out of my room. "Doctor!" I shouted as he came in.
"What is it?" He asked.
"I don't feel safe."
"I understand that, given what has just happened but we have the police here and everything will be okay." The doctor said as he came over and grabbed my hand. I looked at him.
"What are you doing?" I said as he was holding my hand.
"I am just checking for a pulse." The doctor said.
"You can clearly see that I am breathing." I said as the doctor then looked at his notepad.
"Yes yes, I was just checking your heart rate. You knob!" He said as suddenly he got angry. "No need to snap, Jerry!" He said to himself. I looked at him.
"So when can I get out of here?" I asked him.
"Will you give me a second?" Jerry said as he then snapped at me again.
"Wow dude, I was just asking a simple question."
"Shut up!" The doctor said as he then slapped me across the face. "You will listen to me, I am the doctor." Jerry said as all of a sudden a nurse came in.
"JERRY!" She shouted as she rushed over and grabbed him. "Come take a rest." She said to him as she kissed him on the cheek. Jerry was frustrated with himself.
"Sorry I shouldn't have done that." He said as he kissed the nurse back. I was just confused.
"What is going on?" I said to the doctor.
"You are free to leave." The doctor said as he had given the green light to my departure.

"Oh thank you." I said as I grabbed my coat and began to get ready to leave as the nurse took the doctor's notepad.
"Jerry." The nurse said.
"What!" He said.
"He can't leave, we still need to test his blood." The nurse said.
"Stuff that." Jerry replied as he threw everything on the floor and walked out.
"Sorry sir, you can't leave just yet." The nurse then said to me, I looked at her.
"I understand your concerns but the doctor has signed me off." I said as I got up from my bed and began to walk to the door.
"I'm sorry, but he isn't in the right frame of mind."
"I don't care, I have stuff to do." I said to the nurse as she grabbed me. "Ma'am, can you get off me." I said as I pushed her away.
"Ow!" The nurse said as she fell onto the floor. I rushed over to the door as I saw police officers working on the scene outside my room.
"What happened out here?" I asked the officer.
"You don't want to know about it." He said as he laughed.
"Why are you laughing?" I asked him.
"Sorry, I just found something funny." The officer replied.
"It doesn't seem funny, someone could have died." I said to the officer's face. The officer then changed his tune.
"Sir, I'm going to have to ask you to calm down." He said.
"I haven't done anything." I said as the officer then grabbed my arm.
"You are under arrest for intimidating an officer." He said to me as I was confused. "You are going to spend the rest of the day behind bars." The officer said as I was looking around for a hidden camera or something.

6

I was taken to the police car and then arrived at the police station after a short drive. I was being escorted to the reception desk. I looked at the other man at the desk as he turned around and saw his big grin on his face. "So you have arrived." Billy said. I was still confused.
"Please officer, I haven't done anything, don't do this."
"Is that a threat?" The officer said as we were standing in line behind Billy and his officer. Billy continued to laugh as he kept saying my name over and over.
"George, George, George." He said as the officer escorting him was filling out the paperwork. I was looking at my officer.
"Oh please don't put me in the same cell as him."
"Sir, please be quiet." My officer said as he shocked me with his taser. I slowly fell to the floor and banged my head. Next thing I know I woke up in the middle of a prison cell with half of my clothes off.
"What happened?" I said as I was still holding my head. "Ow!" I let out. I looked around to find a group of men all looking at me. "What have you done?" I asked them. None of them said anything as it was getting colder. "Can I have my clothes back?" The old man with the handlebar mustache threw the clothes at me.
"Here you go princess." He said. Everyone was then laughing at me as I struggled to put my clothes back on. I then got up as all the men came around and grabbed my hand. "You are in for a long time." The old man said as I was just confused at what to do.
"I shouldn't even be here."
"Yeah okay." Another prisoner said as he slapped my butt.
"Please don't do that." I said as the prisoners were all still laughing at me. All of a sudden the cell doors opened.
"Here you go, you monsters." The officer said as he threw in the food for the whole cell. I stood back as I watched all the other prisoners rush to the front and eat the food within seconds. My belly started to rumble.
"As someone who owns a sweet shop, I shouldn't be feeling this hungry." I said as the prisoners turned around and looked at me.
"Why aren't you having any?" One of the prisoners said as they came over.
"I'm not really hungry." I said.
"Oh come on." The prisoner replied as he was sharing his food with me. "Come on, at least take a little bite." The prisoner said, egging me on. "Come on!" He continued to say as I slowly took a bite.
"Oh yes!" I said as I started to digest the piece of bread.
"That's a good boy." The prisoner said as he rubbed my head. I spat it out as it wasn't really tasty. I was then being held hostage as they began kicking me.
"What are you doing?" I said as I had to hold back the tears as they were really hurting me in the balls.
"We do this to all newcomers." One of them said. Then all of a sudden there were a few officers who turned up at the cell door.
"Okay, it's time to hit the showers." One of them said as they began to unlock the cell door.
"My favorite time of the day." One of the prisoners added as he laughed. I looked at him.

"What do you mean?" I said as he winked at me.
"Just don't drop the soap." He continued as I nearly threw up in my throat. Everyone was slowly walking out of the cell and passed the officers. I was hanging to the back of the line as I needed to talk to the officers. I slowly moved forward as I came closer to the officer. I then stopped in my tracks.
"Sir, I shouldn't be here, let alone be subjected to all this abuse." The officer didn't say anything as he pushed me along.
"Come on now." He said as I was trying to hold back.
"Please listen to me sir." I said as the officer didn't say anything. "I am being abused." I continued as I showed him my bruises.
"Sir the showers close in 20 minutes, so I suggest you hurry up." The officer said as he didn't say anything else. I rolled my eyes as I needed to get to the showers. I rushed down the hallway as I turned a corner and into the showers, I saw all the beefy men in their underwear all cleaning each other.
"What the hell is going on?" I said as one of the officers then demanded me to take off all my clothes.
"If you are coming in, you need to take off your shirt and trousers." I rolled my eyes as I began to take off my clothes and gave them to the officer.
"Here!" I said as I went in and covered my penis. I went into the showers as one of the prisoners gave me a bar of soap.
"Here, and get under your arms." He said as he hid something up his butt.
"What are you doing?" I asked him.
"You'll find out later." The prisoner said as he squeezed my hand. All of a sudden a bell went off.
"Okay, time to get out." The officers said as the water suddenly switched off.
"But I wasn't finished." I said as the officer came in and began to pull everyone out.
"Grab some clothes and get out!" He shouted. I looked at the other prisoners who were doing what they were told as they got their clothes back and smuggled soap out of the showers. I rushed to put on my clothes as it was getting cold around my private area.
"Wait for me!" I said as I was slightly behind the rest of the group. One of the prisoners waited for me as the officer looked around the room.
"Hey bub, take this." He said as he passed me a knife.
"What is this?" I said as I dropped it. It fell to the floor and made a loud bang as the officer turned around quickly and saw what was going on.
"HEY!" The officer yelled as he walked towards us. I put my hands up.
"I didn't know about that." I said as the other prisoner turned around as his friends started backing him up.
"It was all that dude." The prisoner supporting him said. The officer pulled out his handcuffs and began to handcuff me.
"I haven't got a clue about this knife." I said as he handcuffed me. "Please listen to me." I said as the other prisoners were giggling. The officers picked up the knife and put it in a paper bag.
"You are coming with me." The officer said as I was being escorted away from everyone else.
"You have just extended your time here bub." The officer continued to say.
"Why aren't you listening to me?" I said as I showed off my bruises to the officer.

"I don't care about that." He said as I rolled my eyes trying to hold onto the walls trying to slow down the escort. "Sir." The officer said as he kept pulling me harder and harder. "You are in a lot of trouble." The officer kept saying.

"Yes, you said several times." I said as we made it back to the holding cell.

"Here!" The officer said as he threw me inside the cell. I fell onto the floor as he locked the door behind me. I managed to turn around as the officer walked off.

"Wanker!" I muttered to myself as I sat up and looked around the cells. I saw all the pillows and blankets from the other prisoners all in their correct positions. "I better not touch their shit, otherwise people will get mad." I said as I accidentally kicked some of the pillows. "Oh shit." I said as I bent down and touched the pillows. I found a pile of drugs under the pillows. I didn't know what to do. The officer then came and unlocked the cell door once more. I dropped the drugs as fast as I could. I then turned around and smiled.

"I don't know what you are smiling for George." The officer said as he let the other prisoners in. I was standing over the pillow as I didn't want to get anyone in trouble. Everyone walked in as I was standing as still as I possibly could.

"Here he is." One of the prisoners said as he walked over to me, I began to get scared but all he did was give me a highfive. "Thanks for taking the wrap on that one." He said. I looked at him confused.

"You know that was a bad thing to do."

"So what." The prisoner said as he pushed me out of the way and went down to his pillows.

"HEY!" He shouted as he was searching underneath the pillows. "Someone's been tampering with my stuff." I began to back away and closer to the wall.

"No, you don't understand." I said as I tried to defend myself. "It was an accident." I continued to say as all the prisoners came closer to me.

"You don't mess with someone's drugs." One of the other prisoners said.

"It was a mistake." I repeated as one of the prisoners pulled out something from his pillow case. "I hope you enjoy this." He said as he pulled the knife out and began threatening me. "You give back the drugs now or you will get it." He said.

"I haven't done anything." I replied as the officers were doing nothing. All of a sudden the knife pierced through my skin. "Ow!" I said as I felt my stomach. I fell to the floor. "Why?" I asked as the prisoners were all laughing.

"That's what you get, you cunt." One of the prisoners said as I was bleeding a lot.

"Please get some help!" I said as I was slowly losing breath. The prisoners all laughed except from one in the corner.

"I think we should get some help." He said as he put up his glasses.

"Oh come on Darren, you always have to ruin our fun."

"But he is someone two and he probably has a loving family outside of the prison." Darren said as he ran to the door of the cell and began to call for help. "HELP HELP!" He shouted.

"Someone has been stabbed." He said as I was still choking on my own blood. The officers came in as everyone was forced against the walls.

"Okay okay, everyone stay back." The officer in charge said as Darren was trying to protect himself as he had made a ton of enemies. All the prisoners were looking at Darren as I was getting assisted. "You are going to be okay!" The officer said as he got me up and the other officer put my arm around his neck.

"We are going to get you to the hospital bay." He said as they were rushing me down the hallway. "Out of the way." They said as I was not awake. They placed me down on the bed as the doctor began to look at what was going on.
"Well we are going to need to remove this." He said as he was acting jokily.
"Are you sure you are a real doctor?" The officer said to him.
"Of course." The doctor said as his eyes were acting shifty. "Okay you can leave now, I can handle it from here." The two officers left the room as he then took off his mask. "Remember me George?" The doctor said.
"Billy?" I said as one of my eyes opened slowly.
"Yes." He said.
"What are you doing here?" I asked him.
"I am here to stop you."
"I haven't done anything." I replied as he was sewing through my chest.
"I know what you have done with Amy." Billy said.
"I don't know who you are talking about." I said as Billy then showed me more pictures.
"Is this you?" I looked at the pictures.
"I don't know." I said as he shoved the pictures in my face. "I don't know what you are talking about?" I said as Billy then pulled out something from his pocket.
"Here, I have a recording of you and Amy going at it on the counter of your shop." I began to sweat buckets.
"Okay, okay, so what do you want?" I asked him.
"I want you to do a job for me." Billy said.
"What job?"
"I need you to get some stuff from around the prison." Billy announced as someone knocked on the door. "Come in!" Billy said as a big strong man came in. "I'm glad you are here." Billy said to the man who came in and sat down on a chair.
"Anything for you boss." He said as he pulled out a screwdriver and hammer out of his pockets. "Here." He continued to say. I looked at him.
"This is your new helper." Billy said. "This is Micheal." Billy continued as Micheal put out his hand as I went to shake it.
"So what do you want me to do?"
"Well I heard someone is carrying around a spare set of officer keys and I want you to get them." Billy said as Micheal was listening as well. I slowly sat up on the hospital bed as I had recovered from Billy's dodgy operation.
"Look, I don't really want to get involved in all this prison stuff." I said as Billy kept pointing at the pictures.
"I will release them." Billy threatened as I didn't know what to do. I took a big deep breath as I then said.
"Okay, I will do one job and one job only." I said as Billy smiled. Micheal looked at me.
"Okay, I know a couple of good starting spots." He said as I hopped off the bed and slowly walked out of the medic bay.
"I think we should start in the woodwork room." Micheal said as we were both walking back to our cells.
"Oh okay, but I can't do it for a while because my arm is still hurting." I said.

"Don't be a wimp." Micheal replied as he took the crutch off me. I grabbed onto the wall. He threw the crutch across the hallway as I was holding onto the wall. "This way George." Micheal said as I turned around and saw the officers standing there.
"Okay okay, I'm coming." I said as I limped it back to our cell. We walked in to see Darren sitting in the corner. I sat down next to him as everyone else was sneering.
"Little cunt." One of them muttered.
"Hey, what is up?" I said as I sat down.
"Nothing." Darren said.
"I can clearly see that you are down."
"It's just I shouldn't have helped you. Now everyone hates me."
"I don't hate you." I said as Micheal came over and sat down next to me as well.
"We can use you." Micheal said as I looked at him.
"No!" I said firmly.
"Yes!" Micheal said as he put his foot onto my foot and pushed down. "Are you going to do the woodwork tomorrow?" Micheal asked Darren.
"I haven't really decided yet." He said.
"Oh you will." Micheal replied as he leaned in on Darren.
"I don't want to do anything stupid." Darren said as I stopped hugging him.
"You work for me now." Micheal said as he slipped him a sharp blade from under his prisoner outfit and into Darren's hands. "See, here is what you are going to do." Micheal said as he whispered in Darren's ear as I was just sitting there holding my arm as it was still hurting.
"I really don't want to." Darren said as he was getting quite nervous.
"Come on Mike, you can't just get everyone involved in yours and Billy schemes."
"Quiet you!" Micheal said to me as he was still trying to get Darren involved with him.
"Okay okay." Darren suddenly said as he got up and looked at all the prisoners laughing at him.
"Here comes the baby bunch." One of the prisoners announced as they looked at the 3 of us.
"Oh, up yours!" Micheal said as he rushed over to defend Darren. "This guy is going to be a star." He said as I was just sitting down on the bench looking confused. I tried to look for a clock as I knew it was going to be a long time in prison, but I couldn't spot one. I then laid down as I was getting sleepy and couldn't deal with the abuse that the other prisoners were saying to me and the other two. I put my head down and try to ignore the noise. Meanwhile Micheal was edging on the other prisoners. "Come on." He said as he knew Darren was carrying a dangerous weapon. I fell asleep after 10 minutes of just looking at the ceiling as it was quite hard to get a good night's sleep here as all the other prisoners were still making noise. The officer walked by and said.
"Come on guys, lights out." He said as he flicked the light switch.
"HEY!" Several prisoners said as they all tried to find their sleeping position. The night was long and cold as I had very little to cover myself with. I woke up as the lights were still out. I looked around as the prisoners were sneaking around and trading stuff with each other.

7

All of a sudden the lights came on as an overhead alarm began ringing and said. "Surprise inspection." I was shocked as I didn't know what was happening. All the prisoners were rushing to the two toilets with their things as they began to start flushing stuff down the toilets. The officers came rushing in as my eyes were still hurting from the flash of light coming on without knowledge. I looked around to see if I could find Darren or Micheal but the officers were already doing their strip searches. I slowly got up and walked over to the wall as one of the officers came over.
"You know how this goes." The officer said as I stood there in silence as he began to go all over me.
"Just do it quickly." I said as I closed my eyes and just thought about Amy and everything else on the outside world. I looked the officer in the eye as he was going up and down my leg over and over.
"Okay, all done." The officer said as he finished patting me up and down as I was worried it was going to be much worse.
"Oh is that it?" I said as the officer looked confused.
"What were you expecting, a massage?" He said. I laughed as he moved onto the next prisoner. I then began to walk back to my bed as I was getting cold. I sat down as I put the blanket back over me.
"Officer, can you turn up the heating?" I asked. The officer turned around and looked at me.
"We don't have heating in here." He said as I looked confused.
"What do you mean?" I said.
"We don't have any heating in this prison, what's hard to understand?" The officer said.
"Oh sorry, I am just cold." I said as I stood up and began to do some jumping jacks to keep warm. Everyone in the cell looked at me.
"Sit down George!" One of the officers asked. "This isn't play time."
"But I'm cold." I said over and over. All of a sudden one of the other prisoners gave me their blanket.
"Here!" He said as I looked at him and smiled.
"Thank you." I said as I took the blanket and put it over me. "My name is George by the way." I said to him.
"I know, the officer just called it out." The prisoner replied as we both laughed. I looked at him in his bright blue eyes. "My name is Simon." The prisoner said as I nodded my head.
"You are very nice Simon." I replied to him.
"Why, thank you!" Simon said as he came over and sat down next to me. The officers were still doing their strip searches on everyone as me and Simon were getting cozy underneath the blankets.
"HEY!" One of the officers shouted. "No making out." He said.
"Why not?" I asked him as Simon suddenly kissed me.
"Because!" The officer said.
"Because what?" I said. I then kissed Simon on the lips as we began to make out in front of the whole cell. The officers came over and ripped us apart.
"NO!" He demanded as he hit me and Simon.

"Ouch!" I said as the officer said.
"You know that isn't allowed here." The alarm then went off in the prison.
"It's time for breakfast." One of the officers said as I winked at Simon as he had passed me a key through kissing him. I got up and walked over to the cell door as Darren and Micheal then followed me out. The officers were then escorting us to the lunch hall as I slipped the key from my mouth to my hand. I then passed it to Micheal all without the officers catching on.
"Here we go boys." I said as Micheal then headed for the bathrooms as I and Darren went into the lunch hall and went up to the counter and asked for some service. "Hello, can I have a sausage sandwich?" I asked the lunch lady. She then passed it to me as she was smoking and coughing all over the food. "Thank you."
"That would be 50 pence." She replied as I handed her the money. I then walked away as Darren was still on the counter as he was still deciding what to order. I sat down next to some of the prisoners as they looked at me funny.
"So what's your problem?" One of them asked.
"Nothing." I replied as I sat down and smiled at them.
"What are you laughing at?" He questioned me.
"Oh, it's just, I'm getting out of here." I said suddenly as I then realized what I said. "No, I didn't mean that." I said as suddenly one of the officers walked over and said.
"Did I just hear correctly?" He said as I then began to sweat.
"No, no, I said, I'm getting out of the lunch hall." I said as I tried to deflect from what really happened. "I love this place." I said as I was chewing through my sausage sandwich. Darren then came over with his chicken and potatoes. "I see you have a lot of food." I said as Darren sat down.
"I am hungry." He said as the officer then walked away.
"Okay okay, but I will be watching you." The officer said.
"So, how are you getting out?" The prisoner asked as he wanted to get involved.
"Keep this on the down low but we are planning a riot in the woodwork shop in the coming days." I said as Darren was enjoying his food.
"I want in!" The prisoner said as I looked at Darren.
"I don't know dude."
"I will tell the officers." The prisoner threatened as he began to call the officer over.
"No, don't!" I said as the officer walked over.
"What's up?" He asked as he was talking to the officer privately. "Oh okay." The officer said as he then turned around and walked away from the table and rushed out of the lunch hall.
"So what did you say?" Darren asked the prisoner.
"I said there was going to be a fight in one of the cells."
"Oh." I said.
"I'm Roger!" The prisoner said as he put his hand out for me to shake it.
"Nice to meet you Roger. I'm George, and this is Darren." I said.
"Well you are going to need these." Roger said as he pulled out 2 screwdrivers from his back pocket. Darren took them.
"Oh thanks." He said.
"So when is this big heist going to happen?" Roger asked.
"Oh just 2 days from now." I said.

"Cool." Roger said as he was writing it down on his napkin. Darren then finished his meal and took mine. He then put his tray back on the cleaning sink. All of a sudden he was attacked from behind by a number of prisoners. I looked over as I couldn't believe what was happening.
"DARREN!" I shouted. Roger then grabbed my hands as he took back the screwdriver and stabbed them through my hands. I let out the loudest scream I ever produced as Darren fell to the floor. The officers rushed over and pulled the prisoners away from Darren as he only managed to get a few cuts and bruises. I looked at my hand as there was tons of blood pouring out. I then began to start feeling dizzy as my other hand was trying to pull out the screwdriver from my hand as Roger was laughing.
"You really think it's that easy?" Roger said as the officer then took him away back to the holding cell. I tried to lift my hand up from the table but couldn't in case it would cause more damage. The officers were radioing for medical assistance as I sat in pain. All of a sudden Billy came rushing in with his first aid kit as he ripped out the screwdriver out of hand as I screamed in pain. Everyone else was looking at Billy as he then put special things on my hand as I tried to get the feeling back into my hand. He then whispered into my ear.
"What are you doing?" He said as I looked at him.
"I'm sorry, I didn't know he was going to attack me." I said.
"You need to complete the mission by the end of tomorrow otherwise I will leak those photos."
"I'm doing all I can." I replied as Billy gave me some tablets. He then grabbed me and we walked out of the lunch hall. Micheal then came back from the bathrooms as he saw my hand wrapped in bandages.
"What happened?" He asked.
"Just a misunderstanding." I said as Billy gave me more tablets to disgust. Micheal then unwrapped the bandage. "What are you doing?" I said as he wanted to have to look at it.
"Oh sorry." Micheal said.
"You're hurting my hand." I replied as Billy was talking to Micheal.
"We need to get this job done with professionals."
"There are no professionals." Micheal announced as Billy was getting angry. Micheal then looked into the lunch hall as Darren was resting on the benches. Micheal then began to walk towards Darren as the officers were doing their rounds. "D, we need to have a group meeting." Micheal said in his ear.
"Can you give me a second to rest." He said as he was just beaten up.
"Oh yes." Micheal said as Billy and myself were walking back to our cell as we needed a secret location for us to meet. We sat and waited for Micheal and Darren as they were just coming along 5 minutes later. Micheal and Darren came walking in as Darren was still holding his hand.
"Okay gang, we need to discuss the current ideas."
"Well I didn't expect them to come along and start bullying us." Darren said as I was still trying to stop the bleeding from my hand.
"Okay okay, I'm going to have to get involved." Billy said.
"But, you are the prison doctor." I said as all of a sudden he pulled out a spare set of prisoner clothes.
"I can be whoever I want to." Billy said as he then managed to change clothes as everyone else was looking at the officer walking by.
"Wow, you did that so fast." I said as myself, Darren and Micheal all looked back.

"So what is the plan Billy?" Micheal asked.

"Okay okay!" He said as he pulled out a map from his back pocket. "I want you to go to the workshop tomorrow and try to get as many tools as possible." Billy said.

"Oh okay." Micheal said as he wrote his instructions down.

"What about me chief?" Darren said.

"I want you to hack into the main security camera and stop them from seeing what we are doing!" Billy said as he pulled out a laptop from underneath the bench.

"Oh okay." Darren replied as he put on his glasses. Billy then turned to me.

"George. I want you to stay here and rest your hand."

"But then how am I going to get out of this place?"

"I will give you a whistle to let you know we are nearly there." Billy said.

"Oh okay." I said as I was resting up my hand. Billy and Micheal walked out of the cell as I sat there with Darren as he was trying to hack into the security cameras.

"Oh this is hard." He said as I was still digesting the tablets Billy gave me.

"Can I have a look?" I said as Darren passed me the laptop as one of the prison officers walked past the cell to see us chatting.

"Ok this is easy." I said as Darren was looking at me confused.

"If you are so smart, why don't you do it then?" Darren said.

"Oh okay." I said as I used my other hand and began to search through the security cameras to find out where Micheal and Billy were.

"So what should we do?"

"Go help them in the workshop room?" I suggested as Micheal and Billy were walking towards the workshop room with screwdrivers in hand. They entered the room as an officer asked to search them.

"Morning boys, just a little routine check."

"Oh yes." Billy said as he shoved the screwdrivers up his butt. The officer then did a quick check over their bodies as I was watching from my cell. Micheal and Billy were then let into the workshop as Micheal then pulled out the two screwdrivers from Billy's butt.

"Okay, here we go." Micheal said as they headed towards the back wall of the workshop and began to start unscrewing the screws to the air vent. All of a sudden there was an alarm. Billy and Micheal looked at each other as the officers then shouted,

"GET OUT!" Micheal and Billy didn't move as they didn't want to leave. They then began to sneak through the air vents. I was looking through the security cameras as all of a sudden I spotted a fire starting in the kitchen.

"Oh shit." I said to myself as I flipped through the cameras to see Darren running down the hallways as all of the other prisoners were walking the other way. The officer pushed him.

"What do you think you are doing?" The officer questioned Darren. "Don't you hear that alarm?"

"I do but I need to get something from my cell." Darren said as he was pushing back the officer.

"I don't care, there is a fire and that means it's time to get out before we all burn to death." The officer said as he was pushing back. Darren then gave up as he knew he had to get out so he wouldn't look suspicious.

"Okay okay, it was only a few playboy magazines anyway." Darren said to himself as he turned around and followed all the other prisoners. All of a sudden I got up from my cell and hid the laptop underneath the bench as the officer was doing his final call.

"Sorry sorry!" I said as I got up and rushed out of the door of the cell.
"What took so long?" The officer asked as I was just getting my breath back.
"I was just sleeping and didn't hear the alarm." The officer rolled his eyes as he could tell I was lying.
"Oh okay, you know what to do." He told me.
"Yes, out to the garden." I said. I walked through the hallways as I could smell the smoke and fire coming down the halls. "I hope everyone made it out already." I said to myself as I turned into the garden. I then saw Darren shaking. I walked over to him. "What's the problem?" I said as I tried to keep him calm.
"I didn't do it." He said.
"Do what?" I asked.
"Complete the mission." Darren replied as I tried to calm him down.
"You didn't fail anyone." I said to him.
"I did."
"Who?" I asked.
"Myself." Darren continued to say as I was looking down.
"You didn't." I said.
"And Billy." He continued to say. "He is going to hit us." Darren continued.
"No he isn't." I said as I looked around the garden. "Where are Billy and Micheal?" I asked.
"I haven't seen them." Darren replied as the fire raged on.

8

Meanwhile Billy and Micheal were still inside, trying to get the air vents screws off as the fire raged on. "We need to get out." Micheal said as Billy was still going at it.
"No, there is only one way out for us and that's through the air vents." Billy said as he ripped off one of the screws.
"The only way out for us is in a body bag." Micheal said as he ripped Billy away from the vents.
"NO!" He shouted as Billy then stabbed one of the screwdrivers through Micheal's foot.
"OW!" Micheal screamed as he took in a ton of smoke down his throat. He began to choke as Billy pushed Micheal down to the floor as he ripped the air vent off.
"Are you coming or not?" He asked Micheal as his foot bled so much it was dripping out of his shoe.
"Are you kidding?" Micheal said as he got on all fours and began to crawl after Billy. The smoke was catching up to them as the fire raged on. They dashed through the vents as quickly as they could. Billy led the way. The smoke was coming towards them all of a sudden as they turned the corner. "Why did you think coming into the air vents was a good idea?" Micheal asked as the smoke was coming closer and closer to both of them.
"I didn't expect there to be a fire did I?" Billy rebutted as he took his shirt and covered his mouth, he then began to crawl into the smoke. Micheal was shocked as he didn't know what to do. All of a sudden he then began choking.
"Bill." Micheal said as he couldn't really breathe. He fell to the floor of the air vent as Billy went on leaving him behind.
"Bye Mike! It was nice knowing you." He said as he quickly turned around to looked at Micheal's corpse lying in the air vent. All the smoke came around him and made him disappear. Billy continued to crawl on as the vents were getting covered in smoke. He then looked down at the vents as one of the ways led to the chief officer's office. He then kicked it open as he then dropped down and landed on the desk. He then looked around as there was little smoke in the room. He then searched through the office as he tried to find the prison cell keys. "Where are they?" He said as he began to kick stuff around. All of a sudden someone opened the door. It was a firefighter.
"What are you doing here?" He said as Billy grabbed the lamp off the officer's desk.
"Piss off." Billy said as the smoke and fire began to start sneaking into the office.
"You need to get out." The firefighter said.
"Fuck off." Billy replied as he began to start throwing stuff at firefighters as they used his hose and put out the fire with his water. "Go away." Billy repeated as Billy moved closer with the lamp.
"I will hit you." Billy said as all of a sudden a second firefighter came rushing in.
"Oh please, the building is on fire, we don't have time for this shit." The firefighter said as his buddy walked away and went to fight the fire in another part of the prison. "Put that lamp down." The firefighter said as Billy looked at him.
"Fuck you." He said as he threw it. It hit the firefighter in the head and cracked his helmet.
"Oh god." He said as he took in a whole lot of smoke. "Please get some help." The firefighter said as Billy was holding his breath. The firefighter then dropped to the floor as Billy then rushed over and picked up the helmet off him.

"Fuck you." Billy said as he put the helmet on and grabbed some tape to tape up the hole that he made. He walked over the firefighters body as he grabbed the oxygen tank from his back. The other firefighters all looked at him as he was rolling through the hallways as the firefighters were scared of touching him.
"Sir, you have to leave." The firefighter said.
"Fuck you." Billy repeated to them as he walked through the hallway as the fire raged on. All of a sudden the ceiling began to collapse around Billy and the firefighter. "Fuck!" Billy said to himself as a huge iron beam landed on one of the firefighters. Billy was trying to get over the large beam but it was too hot. The firefighter came rushing back.
"What are we going to do?" Billy asked the firefighter.
"We are going to have to call for backup to cut through this beam."
"But what about the smoke?" Billy asked as there was more smoke than oxygen in the air.
"We just have to take it." The firefighter said as he had given up. All of a sudden we both looked up and saw that the iron bar above was also collapsing. "I don't think there is a way out." The firefighter said as unexpectedly the iron bar fell down and completely squashed the firefighter, it also landed on Billy's leg. "OW!" He said as he couldn't move.
"I can't believe this." Billy said to himself as the oxygen tank had all run out. "I'll be back." He suddenly said with his last dying breath. As Darren and I were still in the yard with all of the other prisoners. There was a loud explosion.
"Stay calm everyone." One of the officers said. All of a sudden one of the officers came by and began to start to roll call everyone. He was ticking everyone's name off the list.
"Where is Billy, the doctor?" He asked several of the other officers.
"I haven't seen him in days." One of the officers said.
"Oh, I guess he is gone." The officer said as he crossed the name off the list.
"Oh, I better tell the governor." One of the other officers said as he pulled out his phone and began to call the governor.
"So what are we going to do?" Darren asked me.
"I don't know, maybe they let us all go."
"Are you stupid, we are going to be transferred to another prison or something." Darren said as he was getting nervous by the second.
"Why are you getting so nervous?" I asked him.
"Because the fire investigation is going to find out that I started the fire." I looked Darren in the eye.
"What!" I said. "Why?"
"Because I couldn't let Billy and Micheal control me." Darren said. I then pushed him away.
"They were the only way out of this hellhole."
"No they weren't." Darren said as he then took his glasses off and threw them down to the floor. "You think you are so big, George, but you are not." He said as he then dashed towards me. He hit me right in the stomach as I went up against the wall.
"Ow!" I said as the other prisoners were still watching the fire burn through the prison.

9

Suddenly there was an alarm that went off. "Okay okay." The officer said with a megaphone in hand. "We need everyone to get into the groups they were put in when they were sentenced because we are about to ship you off to other prisons." Meanwhile me and Darren were still fighting as no one seemed to be paying attention to the pair of us. One of the officers suddenly came rushing down as he spotted us.
"HEY!" He shouted. "Stop that you two." He continued as he grabbed Darren and pulled him off. I was laying on the floor as blood came out of my mouth.
"You cunt." I shouted at Darren.
"HEY!" The officer replied. "Enough of that." He continued while restraining Darren. "Get in line right now!" He demanded as he took Darren away. I slowly got up.
"Okay sorry." I said as I walked over to the 5th line. The man in front of me turned around.
"Howdy." He said.
"Hello." I replied politely.
"My name is Jimmy." The man said.
"Oh, my name is George." I replied.
"So what are you in for?" I asked Jimmy.
"I'm not really sure." He replied.
"Oh." I said as the officers were then leading the line out to the prison bus. "So where are we going?" I asked Jimmy.
"I'm not sure." He replied.
"Not a man of many words are you?" I said to him. He shrugged his shoulders as I stepped onto the prison bus. I took a seat at the back of the bus as Jimmy was sitting against the window. "So do you wanna be friends?" I asked him. He didn't reply as the bus door closed. "Do you like being in prison?" I asked him as the bus began to drive off. Jimmy wasn't saying a word as he was looking out the window watching the prison go up in flames. "Okay." I said as I turned away from him as I knew he didn't want to say anything. "Well if you ever need anything I will be here." I said as I tried to fistbump him but he was not responding. "Oh, okay." I said as I turned back around and looked at the other prisoners. The bus drove off as we made it on the motorway. The 2 officers onboard were walking up and down the middle aisle as they were checking nothing illegal was going on. I then asked the officer. "Where are we going?" I said in a flash.
"Your new prison." The officer replied.
"I know that but where?"
"I can't disclose that information." He said.
"But what about my family?" I said.
"Your family will be updated in due course." The officer said as he walked away. All of a sudden Jimmy got up from his seat. He went over to the officer and suddenly punched him. He fell into a number of other prisoners. The driver looked around, taking his eyes off the road. He then swerved off the motorway. All the prisoners were scared, holding onto the metal bars in front of them to make sure they didn't get hurt. The driver was trying to take control but it was too late. All of a sudden he crashed the bus into a tree. The passengers went flying as I managed to hold

myself back and only fall under the seat. Then all of a sudden I felt my left leg being tugged on. I didn't know what was going on.
"Stop!" I said, trying to kick them off me.
"We need to get out." The voice said as he broke through the glass window. The window smashed as glass went everywhere.
"Ow!" I said as he twisted my foot. He was pulling me out as I went over the glass spikes that covered the window. He placed me on the grass as the bus was on its side. The prisoners and officers were still trying to get themselves together and get out.
"I need to go in and help!" The man said as I grabbed his foot.
"Please don't, it's going to blow up."
"I have to." He said as he turned around and I saw his face.
"Jamie?!" I said surprised as I was trying to recover as several other prisoners were running off. I was laying on the grass with my ankle twisted and my back broken. Jamie went back in through the window as he was trying to get more prisoners out. All of a sudden I noticed there was smoke coming from the front of the bus. I shouted. "Jamie, get out, the bus is on fire!"
Suddenly a small spark came from the engine. Jamie didn't reply as I tried to sit up. One of the prisoners came over and began to start stealing the medical supplies from the bag that was next to me. "HEY!" I yelled as I tried to slap him. "Stop." I said with a demanding tone in my mouth as all of a sudden I grabbed his leg and he tripped over, spilling the supplies all over the floor. He then proceeded to kick me in the face. "What are you doing?" I asked him.
"I need to get out of here." He said as I was trying to be a good citizen. All of a sudden Jamie came back out the window with another person.
"Here." He said as I limped over to him and tried to patch him up. It was a police officer. All of a sudden his radio went off.
"Hello?" I said as I picked it up.
"Who is this?" The voice said. "Where is officer 215?" The voice asked.
"There has sort of been an accident and the prison bus we were traveling in has crashed and everyone is hurt." I said.
"Oh!" The voice replied concerned. "Where are you located?" The radio operator asked. I began to look around as all I could see was trees and bushes.
"I don't know sir. All I see is a forest." I said.
"What about the road?" The radio operator said as I slowly got up and went over and saw it was a dusty motorway.
"It's just a motorway sir, a long stretch, I can't see any cars."
"What's the license plate of the bus?" The radio operator asked as I turned around to look at it.
"R….5" I said as all of a sudden the engine went up in flames. I jumped as the blast was too much and I had to duck to get away from all the metal and items flying towards me. I dropped the radio as I fell down. Suddenly a tree collapsed and crushed the radio. I was keeping myself in a small ball position as I was scared at what was going on. All of a sudden I heard a car horn beep as they came to a sliding halt as the fire was raging on and caught onto the trees of the forest. The car stopped as the person pulled out their phone and called for the police.
"One second." They said as they opened their car window and shouted at me. I was laying on the floor about to cry. "Is everyone okay?" He said to me as he rushed out and ran over to me.
"Oh, you are prisoners." He said to me.

"And?" I said as he helped me up. He rolled his eyes and then dropped me. "Oh okay." I said annoyed as I held onto his car. He then dashed into his car and then drove away from the scene as he didn't want to help prisoners. "No! Comeback!" I shouted as the fire was getting hotter and hotter. The car drove off so fast that it must have been speeding. "FUCK YOU!" I screamed as all of a sudden Jamie came and sat down next to me.

"I'm sorry." He said.

"You haven't done anything wrong." I said to him.

"Maybe, if I talked to you, we wouldn't be in this mess."

"No no, it's not your fault at all." I said to him as leaves were burning off the trees. We looked at the long stretch of road and all of a sudden serving police officers came down the road as they spotted the fire. 2 Fire engines were also on the way as me and Jamie got up and waited for the emergency services to come. They pulled over as me and Jamie were waiting. The police pulled down their windows.

"What happened here?"

"I don't recall." I said to the officer.

"Well where are all the other prisoners?" He asked.

"Some ran away as others sadly didn't make it." Jamie said as he showed him the bruises.

"Oh, how many escaped?"

"I don't know." I replied as the firefighters were fighting off the fire.

"Well good for you two for doing the right thing." The officer said.

"Will this get us time off our sentences?" Jamie asked.

"I will certainly let the relevant people know once we get you to your new prison." The officer said as they began to search around the forest for any pieces of evidence.

"So what do we do now?" I asked the officer as Jamie was looking around.

"Well if you just take a seat in the back of my police car, I will just let the other officers know and I will then take you to the new prison myself." He said.

"Oh okay." I said as we both walked to the police car.

"So how long do you think we will get off?" Jamie asked me as we both got into the car.

"Don't tell me you just helped everyone because you wanted time off your sentence." I said.

"Well." Jamie said as I looked at him.

"Oh." I replied. "Well you can be a nice person all the time." I continued.

"But I'm not." Jamie said as he looked around the police car trying to find something to steal. He then grabbed a magazine that one of the officers had left on the passenger's seat.

"What are you going to do with that?" I asked him.

"You just have to wait and see." He said as he chuckled. I was getting concerned.

"What do you mean?" I said as he then hit me.

"Just shut up!" He said to me. All of a sudden an officer came back in and sat in the driver's seat.

"Okay okay, so I will just get myself ready and I will get you to your new prison." The officer said.

10

All of a sudden Jamie then took the magazine and began to start choking the officer. "What are you doing?" I said as Jamie was trying to kill the officer. No one was watching as Jamie was getting away with it. "STOP!" I yelled as I grabbed his arm. Jamie then bit me. "OW!" I said. The officer passed out as Jamie then got out the back seat of the car and opened the front door as he then pushed the officer's lifeless body over to the passenger's seat. I sat in the backseat as I was getting scared. "Jamie, you don't wanna do this." I said as he tried to put the car into drive. I banged on the windows, screaming for help. No one could hear me as Jamie was reversing. He strapped the officer to the passengers chair with tape and rope as he was still trying to get onto the road. "JAMIE!" I shouted as all of a sudden one of the officers turned around and saw what was happening.

"STOP!" He bellowed as he began to dash into the car's way. He was trying to stop the car. I kept banging as Jamie then whacked me with his magazine. I tried opening the door as he locked the door.

"Please let me out, don't drag me into this mess." Jamie then reached around in the glove box as he found a gun.

"Shut up." Jamie said as he pointed the gun at me.

"Woah woah, don't do anything stupid." I said as he then put the car into drive and ran over the cop that was trying to stop the car. He then pointed the gun at the officer in the passenger seat. He then pulled the trigger as he shot the unconscious officer. 'BANG!' is all I heard as I got scared and ducked behind the chair. Blood flew everywhere.

"So you're going to try to fight me now." Jamie said as I was getting scared.

"Please, you don't want to do this." I repeated as he then aimed the gun at my head as he was speeding down the highway. I was just confused on what to do. I turned around to see the police chasing us. I then decided to bang on the back window, trying to tell the police that I wasn't involved. But Jamie slammed on the brakes as the car unexpectedly stopped. The police cars chasing us had to react with seconds to spare. They went all flying over the road as they didn't see it coming. Jamie then turned around.

"SHUT UP!" He shouted at me.

"But I just want to be let go." I said quietly as I began to sweat.

"Too bad." Jamie said as he then shot me in the leg.

"OW!" I let out as I grabbed my leg as the bullet went in deep. "What was that for?" I said as I took off my shirt and wrapped it around my leg trying to stop the blood from leaking out.

"JUST SHUT UP OR YOU WILL GET ONE THROUGH THE HEAD." Jamie shouted at the top of his lungs. He then dropped the gun on the dashboard and proceeded to start the car up once more. There were 2 officers who came out of their police cars and rushed over, trying to open up the back door, trying to get in and stop Jamie. The car then drove off as they fell to the floor. I was still holding onto my leg as blood was coming out the sides of the shirt that I wrapped around it.

"Please, I need help." I suddenly said as I then grabbed the officer's dead body that was still laying in the passenger's seat.

"What are you doing?" Jamie asked as he then whacked my hand.

"Please, I just need some bandages." I said as I began to feel dizzy and ill.

"No!" Jamie said as he then did a hard corner on the road. The police were still following us as I turned around and looked out the back window. Jamie then saw a ramp. "Watch this!" He then boasted as I saw what he was about to do.
"No, please, we will both be killed." I said.
"So what." Jamie continued without a care in the world as he pressed further on the gas pedal. I then took a big breath as the car then went flying over the ramp. I kept my head down as I knew what was going to happen. All of a sudden the car had crashed into a building as Jamie was squished between his seat and the building. He died on the spot. I was under a pile of metal as I couldn't feel my legs. The police came rushing onto the scene as they were still chasing us.
"Everything is going to be okay." One of the officers said as they tried to open the door. I was unable to understand what was going on. The officers broke through the window and grabbed my legs trying to pull me out. "What's that smell?" One of the officers asked as they tried to get me out of the car.
"I think it's the engine." One of the other officers said as the firefighters arrived on the scene and started putting out the fire before cutting me out of the back seat.

11

Everything was then a blur as I slowly woke up from the coma on the hospital bed. "What happened?" I said to the nurse.
"Sir, you are lucky to be alive." The nurse replied.
"Oh, why what happened?" I asked the nurse.
"Well we had to get rid of some of your left leg." The nurse said as she pulled off the blanket that I was under. I saw that my left leg was slightly shorter than my right.
"Oh." I said as I didn't know what to say. "So what happens now?" I asked the nurse.
"I will let the doctor explain everything to you." She said as she began to walk out.
"No, you can't leave." I added as I was looking at the missing piece of my leg. The doctor then walked in.
"George, my man, you are lucky to be alive." He said.
"But doctor, what about my leg?" I asked him.
"Well I'm sorry we had to do that, but it was necessary to get you out of the car."
"It's okay." I said as I understood that it was needed. "So what happens now?" I asked the doctor.
"We are going to get you some crutches for you to use until we get someone to make a prosthetic leg for you to use." I then began to tear up as I then realized that I wasn't able to do so many things anymore. "Don't get upset." The doctor said as he gave me some tissues. "I will order some therapy for you." He continued as I was just confused at everything.
"What about Jamie?" I asked the doctor.
"Who?" He said. "No one else survived the car crash." He then added.
"Oh." I said stunned as I then began to cry over everything. All of a sudden one of the prison officers that was looking after me came into the hospital room and said,
"George, I'm sorry you have to go through all of this." The officer said as I pointed at my leg. "I'm sorry you lost your leg." He continued as he came over and sat down on the chair beside me.
"What will happen to me? Will I go back to prison?" I asked.
"Well I have talked it through with other officers and what you did when the prison bus flipped over was very good. And the fact you had nothing to do with Jamie taking the police car. I had let the judge know and he has decided to quash your sentence completely." He said. I looked at him.
"So I am a free man?" I asked.
"Yes." The officer continued as he then pulled out a box from underneath the bed. "Here is all the stuff we took from you when we arrested you." He said as he took out the stuff and gave it back to me.
"Thank you, I guess." I said as I began to start looking through the stuff the officer had delivered to me. I was then confused. "This isn't my stuff." I said to the officer as I showed him a picture of the man and his family. "Come on, this clearly isn't me." I explained as the officer was shocked.
"Oh sorry." He said as he took everything back from me. "I'm so sorry." He continued as the doctor came back in.
"George, I have something to tell you." He said. I looked at him, scared.
"What?" I asked him.

"We also found something on your brain, when we were in the operating room." I continued to look at him.
"What do you mean?" I asked him.
"We think we found a tumor on your brain."
"No!" I bellowed as the doctor asked me to quiet down.
"Please keep it down for the other patients."
"Am I going to die?" I then asked the doctor.
"I can't comment on that." He said as the officer was listening to everything. He then grabbed my hand.
"Everything is going to be okay." I then pulled my hand away as I was confused. The officer then pulled out something from his pocket. "Here!" He said as he gave me a card with his number on.
"My name is Dermot, and I will always be here for you."
"But why?" I asked him.
"Because my dad had cancer and we did nothing and I miss him everyday."
"Oh, I'm sorry to hear that." I said as he then grabbed his hand once again. "Well Dermot, you will always have a friend in me." I said as the doctor walked away. Me and Dermot looked at each other as I looked into his deep blue eyes. "You have lovely eyes by the way." I said to him.
"Thank you!" The officer said as he came closer and closer. "You have something on your lips." He said as he came closer and closer as he wiped it off my face. "You are so handsome." He said to me as all of a sudden, I pulled him in and we kissed. The door suddenly opened to see me and Dermot making out.
"George!" The voice cried as I pushed Dermot off me. I looked up and saw who it was.
"AMY!" I replied back as I wasn't expecting her to be here. "What are you doing here?" I asked her.
"I heard you were involved in that prison crash that was on the news and I wanted to come see you, but I can see you have someone else here." She said as she reached for the door.
"No, please!" I said, trying to get her attention as I slammed my fist on the bed. "AMY!" I said as I really wanted to explain what had happened. "AMY!" I screamed once more as Dermot was looking at me.
"So I guess you don't like me." He said.
"Not now." I said as I was trying to ignore Dermot. I grabbed the crutch and tried to chase after Amy, but I couldn't get up. "AMY!" I shouted once more as one of the nurses came over and said.
"Please sir, other patients are trying to sleep."
"I understand that but she isn't listening to me."
"Please sir, just respect others." The nurse continued as I tried to follow Amy as she waited for the lift. Dermot was still sitting on his chair in the medical bay as he was confused.
"Amy, please, let me explain." I said as I caught up with her.
"What, you got 5 seconds to explain." Amy said.
"He came onto me." I replied. "I'm not gay and I have always loved you."
"Oh please, we were a hook up in your store which has gotten out of control."
"No, you don't understand!" I said as Amy turned around and saw that half my leg was missing.
"I'm sorry about your leg." Amy jokily said as she stepped into the lift.

"Amy, please!" I said one last time as suddenly I fell to the floor as I lost my balance. Amy stepped into the lift as she didn't care.
"You don't mean anything to me anymore." She said as she flipped the bird at me. The lift door started to close. "Oh and one more thing." She added as I looked up. "I'm pregnant with your child." I was stunned.
"No, that can't be, we used protection." Amy laughed as the nurse rushed over to assist me.
"Is everything okay?" The nurse said to me as I slowly got up.
"AMY!" I shouted once more as the lift had gone down. I pushed the nurse away after I thanked her for picking me up. "I'm just not in the mood." I said.
"Well we need to get you back to the medical bed, so they can do more tests on you." The nurse replied.
"NO!" I demanded as I walked over to the lift and called it for myself. "Tell the doctors, I'm out of here." I said as all of a sudden Dermot came out of the room and came rushing over.
"Are you okay?" He said.
"Oh what do you want?" I replied as I hopped into the lift. He followed me as he pushed the button to the ground floor. "No, I'm not okay." I said to him.
"Why?" He said as he grabbed my hand. I tried to pull away but he wouldn't let go. "I love you." He said as I was confused.
"Get off me." I said as I pushed him against the doors of the lift. All of a sudden the lift stopped.
"See what you have done?" I said as I then began to bang on the lift, trying to get it to move.
"You broke the fucking lift." I said as I snapped at him.
"Oh, I'm sorry." He said to me as all of a sudden his radio went off.
"I was chasing the love of my life and you had to ruin it as usual." I said to him as he began to tear up. He picked up the radio as it said,
"Officer Dermot, come in, we need assistance down at the bakery." Dermot looked at the floor as he didn't have the strength to answer the call. "Officer Dermot!" The radio repeated. He didn't say anything as I was looking at him.
"Everything is going to be okay." I said to him as I had a change of heart.
"It's not." He replied as he dropped his radio. He then fell to the floor as he grabbed his chest. "I don't feel very well George." He said as he was panicking.
"Dude, it's going to be okay." I said to him as I hopped over. I continued to bang on the lift trying to make as much noise as possible.
"What's the point?" He said to me as his radio kept going off.
"Dermot!" The radio repeated as I picked it up.
"Hello?" I said to the lady down the line.
"Who is this?" They asked.
"Yes, I am with the officer. He is collapsing and I think he is having a heart attack."
"Where are you?" The lady said.
"Well we are locked in the elevator at the hospital. I'm banging as hard as I can to get some attention but no one is listening." I said.
"Okay okay." The radio woman said. "I will get you some help." She said as she pulled out her phone and began to phone the hospital. "There are people stuck in your elevator and one of them is having a heart attack." She said down the line as I could still hear the radio.

"Oh okay." The person at the hospital said as she then put down the phone to raise the alarm. All of a sudden I could hear the alarms going off in the hospital as they tried to open the lift doors, but they were steeled shut.
"We are coming to get you." The radio said as I was trying to keep Dermot calm.
"Dermot, the people are coming." I said to him as he was still laying on the floor clutching his chest.
"I can't breathe."
"It's going to be okay." I replied to him as I began to start doing CPR on him. All of a sudden I could hear the lift being pulled up and the doors were starting to open. The firefighters had arrived as they used their big heavy equipment to go and open the doors. The doors opened after 5 minutes of loud banging. The medics rushed in with all their equipment. At this moment, I knew it was too late to catch up with Amy as everyone was in my way. I stood there as I watched the medics work on Dermot as I was looking at my watch. The police came in and walked over to me.
"Excuse me sir, do you mind if I asked you a few questions?" The officer asked.
"Umm…okay." I replied to the officer as he got out his pen and wrote stuff down.
"So how did this happen?" He asked me.
"Well I was chasing after my ex and we jumped in the lift to chase after her because I can't go down the stairs because of my leg."
"I see…" The officer said as the medics had taken out Dermot and rushed him into theater. "And how did Officer Dermot get involved?" The officer continued.
"Well he came to deliver some stuff to me because I have just been released from prison!"
"And how did he end up with you in the lift?"
"Well he followed me because he heard all the noise from when me and Amy were arguing."
"And where is your ex now?"
"I don't know." I said to the officer as all of a sudden the lift door closed and the 3 officers were just standing on the outside of the lift as the lift began to start going down. "See what you have done!" I said.
"Sir, no need to raise your voice." The officer replied. "Sir, just calm down otherwise you will be arrested." I rolled my eyes.
"Is this really your game?" I said to them as I stepped away from the officers. The lift went down to the ground floor to the car park as I slowly hopped out the lift.
"Sir, come back here." The officer said as I turned around and pressed the button to send the lift back up. I slowly hopped through the car park as I saw all the cars underneath the hospital. I came across a big black car as the lights switched on. I looked up at the driver.
"You!" I said. I walked over to the driver's seat as they were just sitting there upset. "Hey, what's wrong?" I said to them.
"I thought you were going to be angry with me."
"No, you made your mind up and I accept that." I said to Amy as she unlocked the doors.
"Come round." She said as she pointed to the other seat. I slowly walked around to get to the other side of the car. I got in.
"So why did you wait for me?" I asked her.
"Because." Amy said as she had tears in her eyes. "Because I still love you."
"I love you two." I suddenly said as Amy was in shock.

"But what about that dude?" Amy asked me.
"He came onto me. He was only meant to deliver some stuff to me from the prison, then he came all over me."
"Oh." Amy said as she was shocked. "That also happened to me!" She said. I looked at her.
"You were kissed by a serving police officer?" I asked her. Amy looked at me.
"You can't tell anyone this, but I was raped." Amy suddenly said. I was shocked.

12

"How long ago was this?" I asked her as she was tearing up.
"This was many years ago, way before we met." She said.
"So why didn't you report this to the police?" I asked.
"Are you going to report your kiss?" She asked me. I turned around and ignored her. "I said, are you going to report your kiss?" She repeated.
"Look, I know it is important for me to report it, but it was only a kiss and you were raped which are two different things." I said.
"Why are you defending that monster?" Amy said as I continued to ignore her.
"I told you." I said as Amy then got out of her car and took a big breath in. I looked at her. "Okay okay, I will report him to the police, but yours is so much more serious."
"It doesn't matter how much it was, it was still assault by the police officer." Amy continued as we proceeded to argue around the car.
"Look, please come back into the car and just sit and listen to me." I said to her as Amy was getting more and more stressed. She slowly got herself back into the car.
"Don't even speak to me." She said as she turned on the car and drove off from the hospital parking lot.
I sat there looking around the car as I was watching the landscape and people on the outside move around. Amy was driving around town as she didn't say anything to me.
"Please talk to me." I said to her after a 10 minute break as Amy was still ignoring me. "Where are we going anyway?" I asked her.
"My house." Amy said as she added "Now shut it." She continued as I just sat there in silence. We drove around town for 50 minutes before we arrived at her house. "Okay we are here." She said as she turned off the engine.
"All right." I said as I opened the door and slowly got out using my crutch. Amy then got out the other side and walked around and assisted me.
"George, there is something I need to tell you." She said as we slowly walked towards the front door of her house. I began to worry.
"What is it?" I said as she got out her keys and slowly unlocked the door.
"YOU!" The man shouted as I stood still. "You had an affair with my wife." He continued as I began to sweat.
"No look, it was one night." I said to him.
"Doesn't matter." The man continued as he came out the front door and came over and grabbed my neck.
"OW!" I said as I was pushed against the wall. "Can you stop!" I tried to say as I was choking.
"You are in a whole lot of trouble." The man said as Amy stood there and laughed at me.
"Help me Amy!" I tried to say as I couldn't really get my words out. All of a sudden Amy jumped on her husband.
"Stop it!" She said as her husband was shocked and confused.
"I thought this was what you wanted?" He said to her.
"Well I don't know." She said as she began to worry. "George is a very nice man." She suddenly said. "And he has been through alot." Amy continued. The husband looked at Amy.
"You still love him don't you." He said.

"Yes!" Amy replied as she dashed over to me as I was sitting on the floor. "How can you not love him?" Amy said.
"You said you loved me, we got married because you said you loved me, we had kids because you said you love me." The husband continued to shout. Amy then grabbed her belly.
"This baby, it isn't yours." She said to him as I kept silent. "It's George's." Amy continued to spill the beans.
"Well you can fuck right off." The husband said as he changed his tune as he went into the house and slammed the door.
"You did that for me?" I said to Amy as she kissed me on the cheek.
"I love you George." She said as she grabbed my hand and placed it on her stomach. "This baby is yours and we are going to be a happy family."
"But where will we live?" I asked her. All of a sudden the husband threw several suitcases out the front door.
"FUCK OFF!" He shouted before closing the door. Amy rushed over to pick up all her clothes.
"We can stay with my sister." Amy continued.
"Oh okay." I said as I looked at her. She came over and helped me up. "So how are we going to get there?" I asked her.
"We can take my car."
"But I thought your husband owned that." I said.
"How do you know that?" Amy asked me.
"Well, I sort of did my research while I was in hospital." I admitted as Amy was stunned.
"So you were stalking me?" She asked.
"No, I just needed a background check." I continued as Amy was getting creeped out.
"Umm…okay?" She said as we walked towards the car. We got into the car as Amy put her suitcases into the back of the car. We then drove off as her husband came back out of the house and shouted at us.
"NEVER COME BACK! YOU SLUT!" I placed my hand onto Amy's knee as we rolled down the road.
"So what is your sister like?" I asked her.
"She is very nice." Amy continued as she smiled at me. "You are special George." She said to me as she honked the horn as traffic began to build up. We went down the highway as I was looking at the cars going past. "I'm sorry about your leg." Amy said.
"Hey, that isn't your fault." I said to her.
"Yer, but I feel bad for it." Amy continued as we pulled up on the house's drive. "Well here we are." Amy said.
"This is my house?!" I said as I woke up from napping.
"What? This is where my sister lives?" Amy continued as she hopped out the car and walked over to the front door. All of a sudden the front door opened as I was still sitting in the car.
"That's my mom." I said to myself as she came out and gave Amy a hug.
"I didn't expect to see you here sis." She said to her.
"Well I have some good news." Amy continued.
"What?" My mom questioned.
"Well I have a boyfriend." Amy said as she rushed over to the car and helped me out.
"This is George." She said as she helped me balance.

"That's my son?" My mother said.
"What?" Amy said. I looked embarrassed. "You didn't tell me this was your mom." Amy said to me.
"I didn't know you were her sister." I replied.
"Oh." Amy said as she then went red faced. My mother was looking at both of us.
"Look, I didn't know this was going to happen!" She said.
"True." I replied as Amy looked at me.
"I..I..I don't know what to think." She said as I began to walk into my house.
"So son, how did you lose your leg?" My mom asked me.
"Oh thanks mom, like you didn't notice." I said to her.
"Well I have been busy running your store." She said.
"Oh yeah, how is the old store going?" I replied to her.
"We have alot of business." She added.
"Oh that is good." I said as I hugged her.
"Yer, but we had to let Sandy go, as she was stealing from the till."
"Oh!" I said as I was shocked. I walked into the front room and sat down. Amy was still standing outside. "AMY!" I shouted as I wanted her to come in. My mother then brought out some family photos.
"See, here is your aunt when you were just a child." She said.
"Oh wow." I said. "I never noticed these photos before." I continued as my mom kept pointing them out. Amy came strolling in as she sat down in the other seat against the wall.
"G, this can't go on." She said suddenly. I looked at her.
"What?"
"We are related, this isn't right." She announced. I looked at her.
"I know finding this out makes you feel uncomfortable." I said as my mother walked out the room and into the kitchen to make some drinks. "Please, I love you Amy, there is no one else I would rather spend my life with then you." I said. She looked at me.
"Just leave me alone." She said to me.
"No please." I continued as all of a sudden I said. "I love you Amy, will you marry me?" My mother brought in some tea as she dropped everything as she came in.
"What do you mean marry her?" My mother asked me.
"Mom, I really love her." I continued as Amy then dashed past my mom and rushed upstairs.
"Oh look what you made me do." My mother said as I was just sitting there as I began to cry.
"No, please Amy." I said as my mother grabbed the broom and mop and began to clean everything up. I was crying as my mother was cleaning up the smashed teapot and cups.
"Son, I think you need to rethink everything." She said to me.
"What do you mean?" I said as I took some tissue and cleaned up my face.
"Well dating your aunt isn't what everyone is doing." She continued.
"Well I am different, you always knew that."
"I know, but my sister, your aunt, is taking it too far." She continued.
"Oh shut up." I replied as I tried to get up from the sofa but I didn't have the strength as I fell down.
"Do you need help?" My mother said as she looked at me.
"Yes please." I continued as she came over with the mop and pulled me up.

"Thanks mom." I said as I came over and gave her a kiss on the cheek.
"Do whatever you want kid, it's your life." She said as I slowly walked upstairs to find Amy.
"AMY!" I shouted as I crawled up the stairs. I went into each room trying to look for her. I couldn't find her until the final room. "What are you doing in my mom's room?" I said to her as I came in.
"This is not a good idea." She said to me as I came in and sat on the bed.
"Why?" I asked her.
"Because it's weird for family reunions." She said.
"Is…that it?" I said.
"I guess." She said as she shrugged her shoulders,
"But no one is going to care about that."
"I care and don't you care about my feelings?" She said.
"I do." I replied as she came over and kissed me on the cheeks.
"You'll find someone." She said as she got up and left me on the bed. I tried to grab her hand as she walked past. She closed the door behind her as I was left in the room all alone. I then heard the front door open and close all within a second. I then made myself comfortable and began to fall asleep on the bed.
"I love her." I said to myself as I closed my eyes. I went to sleep as a headache was coming on. I began to dream about dinosaurs as I needed to take my mind off Amy and everything she brought to me. I slept for over 20 minutes. Before all of a sudden I woke up as if I was having a nightmare. "SHIT!" I said to myself as I woke up. I looked at the clock against the wall. "What time is it?" I said as I was panicking. I tried to get up as I forgot that I lost my leg. "Oh yer." I said to myself. All of a sudden my mother came back into the room.
"Son, this is where you got to." She said to me. I looked at her.
"Where is Amy?" I asked her.
"She left a long time ago, she doesn't want to be with you anymore son, it's time to move on." My mother said as she came in and began to tidy up.
"But I love her!"
"I know you do." She replied to me as I tried to get up from the bed. "But you can't always get what you want in life." She continued. "I loved your dad for so many years before we split and I miss him everyday." She added as I took a second to listen to what she was saying.
"I guess." I said as she helped me up. All of a sudden I looked at my mother as she pulled something out of her back pocket.
"Here." She said. "Now get back to working at the store, I need a holiday." She added as she gave me the keys to the store as she fell down onto the bed.
"I guess, I can afford a couple of days." I said to her,
"Finally." She said as she took a big breath and let it all out. I then began to try to walk out of the bedroom as my mom was getting onto the bed and getting comfortable. I slowly walked out as all of a sudden there was a knock at the door. "Who could that be?" My mother asked as she sighed. She just wanted to rest.
"I will get that." I said to my mom as I began to limp down the stairs. I went to the front door as they continued to knock. "One moment." I said as I quickly looked through the spyhole as I didn't want to look like an idiot when answering the door. I slowly opened the door and noticed it was the mailman. "Oh hello." I said as he passed me the letters.

"Hello there handsome, is your mom in?" He asked.
"She is just upstairs having a sleep."
"Oh okay, don't forget to remind her about bingo tonight at 7." The mailman said as he winked at me. I was confused as I smiled and took a look at the letters.
"Okay." I said as I closed the door. I took all the letters into the front room as I began to read them. "Oh it's my mother's birthday and I completely forgot." I said as I received birthday cards on her behalf, from the mailman. I then proceeded to look at the birthday cards and got myself a little more upset. "I didn't get anything for her birthday, I'm such a bad son." I said to myself as I opened the next card and found it was from me to my mom. "You are the best mother in the world!" It read. "I didn't send this." I said to myself as I was confused. My mother walked into the room. I looked at her. "I thought you were upstairs getting some sleep." I said to her.
"Yes, but I wanted to come see what was in the post today." She said as I was trying to hide the birthday cards from her.
"Do you remember what day it is today?" I asked her.
"Oh no, it's not a bank holiday is it?" She asked. "I have to cash this check." She continued.
"It's not." I said as I gave her the rest of the post, hiding her birthday cards. "Here." I said as I gave them to her.
"Oh thank you." She said as she sat down and began to go through them. She ripped one open and began to read it. "Another bill." She said as she sighed. "I can't afford this." She continued. I looked at her.
"What do you mean?" I asked her.
"Well since I had to cover your store, I had to give up my job at the library."
"Oh!" I said as I was shocked.

13

"Why?" I asked.
"Because I couldn't be in both places at once." She said to me. I was shocked. I then began to start crying. "What's wrong?" She said to me.
"This is all my fault." I said as I then showed her the birthday cards from behind my back.
"Here!" I said.
"What's this?" My mother asked.
"It's your birthday mom, don't you remember?" I said.
"No it isn't, I thought it's not for another couple of months."
"No, it's today." I said as she was shocked.
"Why didn't you tell me?" She asked.
"I forgot as well." I said.
"I have been so busy." I continued as we both laughed about forgetting my mothers birthday. "I love you mom." I said. "Even though I don't show it."
"I know darling." She said as we had a hug. We hugged for over 10 minutes as we just needed to love each other.
"I love you." We both said at the same time. We laughed, we cried as we just needed each other right now.
"So what do we do now?" I said to her.
"Well I think we should get back to your store." My mother said.
"Oh yes, that will be a good idea." I said as I picked up the phone and began to ring for a taxi.
"Hello, can I order a taxi please." I said on the phone as my mom turned on the TV and began to look through what was on.
"Yes, a car will be with you as soon as possible." The man said on the line as I then said.
"Oh and I only have one leg." I continued to him.
"That's okay." The radio operator said. I put the phone down as I then slowly got up and began to walk to the front door.
"I guess it's time to go." I said to my mom as I began to get emotional. "I'm going to miss you." I said to her.
"I am going to miss you two." She replied. I opened the door and slowly walked outside waiting for the taxi to arrive. I must have waited for over 20 minutes before the taxi driver finally arrived. The car pulled up and then honked his horns. I slowly walked up to the car.
"Car for George." The driver said.
"Oh yes, that's me." I said as I got into the car.
"So where are we going?" The driver said.
"Yes, I am going to George's Sugar Shack." I said to the driver.
"Oh that place, it hasn't been open for days." The driver said.
"Oh yes, I have been in a little incident." I continued.
"Oh oh, sorry I didn't know." He continued to say.
"It's okay." I replied as we drove to the store. It must have been 20 minutes of complete silence as we drove from my house to the store.
"Here!" The driver said as I paid him.

"Thank you." I said as I slowly got out of the car and walked towards the store. I got the keys out of my pocket and opened the door. I changed the closed sign to the open sign as I began to walk around the store looking how dirty everything was. "Wow, has no one cleaned this place up?" I asked as I couldn't believe the mess. I grabbed the broom and began to clean up. All of a sudden I turned around as I heard the door open as the bell rang. "You!" I said to the customer. "What are you doing here?"
"I want some sweets." He said.
"I'm not serving you." I said as I went behind the counter. The man came closer.
"I want some sweets!" He demanded as he banged on the counter. I took a deep breath.
"Okay okay." I said, trying to defuse the situation. "What sweets do you want?" I asked him.
"I want some blue mice."
"We don't do blue mice, only strawberries and cream." I said as he was getting angry.
"Look. I don't care, you took my wife, now the best you can do is give me some fucking sweets."
"Well I don't have any blue mice." I repeated. He looked at me with a strange look on his face.
"I WANT SOME FUCKING SWEETS!" He shouted as he then banged on the counter once more.
"Sir, I won't serve you if you continue to be this angry." I said as he then slammed his hand right through the counter and broke it. Sending tons of shards of glass into the selection of sweets. I was shocked as I couldn't believe what happened. I took a step back. "See what you have done now." I said as his hand was bleeding from all the glass shards that entered his hand.
"You have done this." He said threateningly.
"I haven't done anything." I said as I got him a bunch of towels and tried to stop the bleeding.
"Here." I said as he took the tissue of me and began to clean up the mess. "Here, come into the back and we will get that all washed off." I said to him. He shook his head as he was really upset with me. "So what are you going to do?" I asked him. He remained silent as he looked at all the blood dripping out of his hand.
"I hate you." He said as all of a sudden he began to start shaking. I then came out behind the counter and grabbed him.
"Look, I know you hate me, but we aren't together anymore, turns out she was my aunt and it was just awkward." I said to him. He looked at me strangely before fainting onto the floor. I grabbed him before he landed on the floor. I then dragged him into the back room. I got some water from the tap and began to give it to him to drink. He slowly came around as I was checking on the hand and how much blood he was bleeding.
"Get off me." Is all I heard as he pushed me away.
"Dude, you fainted and you really need to see a medic." I said to him.
"Don't tell me who I need to see, I need to see my wife." He said. I suddenly thought.
"If she was my aunt that must mean you are my uncle." I said to him. "Uncle Ray?" I questioned. He looked at me confused.
"I have never heard of that name in my life." He said as he tried to get up. He looked at me and then all of a sudden he came at me and kissed me on the lips. I pushed him away.
"What the fuck was that?" I said to him.
"Don't lie, that's all you wanted from me." He said as he tried to kiss me again.
"What the fuck are you playing at?" I said once more as I threw his hand onto the floor. "Don't ever ask me to do anything ever again." I said as I was slowly walking away. All of a sudden he

grabbed my leg. "What are you doing?" I questioned as I went down and landed on him. He then kissed me once more within a second of falling. He then began ripping off my clothes. I couldn't resist, we then proceeded to get naked and began to start having sex on the floor of my store. "Ray!" I shouted as I was suddenly enjoying it.

"Oh George." He continued as he began to stroke my cock. All of a sudden the front door of the store opened once more. We both looked at each other as I rushed to put on my clothes.

"Coming!" I shouted to the customer as Ray was just laying on the floor with his hard cock out.

"Oh yeah, you go get them, tiger!" He said. I then giggled as I couldn't believe what was happening. I went outside to the front of the store to talk to the customer.

"George." He said as he showed his ID badge. I was shocked.

"Who are you?"

"I'm here to inspect the place."

"What for?"

"For the sale of the place." He said. I was confused. "This place isn't for sale, sorry you are confused." I said as he handed over a piece of paper.

"This is your signature?" He asked. I looked at the piece of paper to discover it was my signature.

"I don't remember signing this." I admitted to him.

"Sorry, I have to follow orders." He said, "And you have signed it, so we are going through with the sale." I continued to look at him confused. "Sir, you have to sign it right now." He said as I took the clipboard and began to read through it.

"Give me the pen then." I said as he handed me the pen. I proceeded to sign it. "Here you go." I said as I threw it back to him.

"Okay good." He said as he looked at my signature. "You don't mind if I have a look around do you?" He asked. I looked at him for a few more seconds as I then noticed the glass all over the floor.

"Umm...do you mind if you give me a couple of minutes." I said as all of a sudden I remember my uncle in the back room. The man nodded his head as all of a sudden a customer came in.

"Excuse me, are you open?" He asked.

"No no, we are just doing some renovations." I said to him as he put on a sad face and closed the door.

"Oh okay." He said as he walked away.

"Is that how you treat all your customers?" The inspector said.

"Well I didn't want them to come in while you are here and I'm still cleaning out the sweets with all this glass." I said as I took the glass shards out of the box.

"Oh okay." The inspector said as he noted that down.

"Do you want some sweets?" I asked the inspector.

"No thanks." He replied.

"So what are you going to do with this place?" I asked him.

"I'm not sure yet, maybe sell it to McDonalds." He said.

"Oh!" I said as I was surprised. "But there is a McDonalds on the other street." I replied.

"But it will create more jobs in the area." He replied.

"Oh okay." I said as I didn't want a fight. The inspector continued to do his rounds and looked around the store.

"We can put an ice cream machine here." He said as I was then walking back into the back room to see Ray sitting on the table. He grabbed my hand and pulled me over.

"Hey baby, who was out there." He said as he kissed me on the cheek. I pushed him away.

"Now is not the time." I said. "I'm losing the store." I continued. Ray was shocked.

"What do you mean?" Uncle Ray replied.

"Someone forged my signature on some sale thing and now the store is up for sale."

"Oh!" Ray replied as he then pulled out his wallet. "I will buy the store back." He demanded.

"No, you don't have to do that." I said.

"I just want to help." Ray continued as he began counting his money. All of a sudden the inspector came into the back room.

14

"Hello, who is this?" He asked as he was taking down the notes.
"Oh this is just my uncle." I said as I didn't want to make anything weird.
"Nice to meet you." The inspector said as he put out his hand for Ray to shake it. "So why are you here?"
"I'm just helping my nephew with the business."
"That's cool!" The inspector replied as I was just standing there in silence. "So are you going to show me around the back?" He asked.
"Just one moment." I said as Ray gave me some cash.
"Here, take this." He said as I was looking at him.
"No no, I can't take this." I said as the inspector was watching.
"Please!" Ray demanded as he pushed the money towards me further. I took the money and threw it on the floor as I began to get angry with Ray.
"HEY!" I shouted at him as the inspector was watching. "You can't bribe me!" I said to him as all of a sudden I spat in his face. The inspector was shocked as Ray slapped me, making me fall towards the floor. The money went everywhere.
"Wow, is this really how you run your business?" The inspector asked as he wrote everything down. I looked at him from the ground.
"No, of course not!" I said to him. "I'm just going through some stuff." I said as he continued to write everything down.
"You don't mind if I check the fridges." He said.
"Sure." I continued as Ray all of a sudden jumped onto me.
"You like that?" He said as he licked his lips. He then began to unzip my pants.
"What are you doing?" I questioned him as he was on top of me. I couldn't move as he was too heavy for me to push off.
"Something I've done before." He said as he then reached down to my penis and grabbed it.
"OW!" I let out. "That hurts." I continued as I tried to kick him off. He was still sticking his mouth on my penis. All of a sudden the inspector came back in.
"WHAT THE HELL!" He bellowed as he spotted what was going on.
"WHY IS HE SUCKING YOUR DICK?" He continued as he dropped his clipboard and walked out of the fire exit. "You will be getting a letter from my lawyers and this place is 100% getting sold." He added as he shut the door behind him. I pushed Ray off me and zipped up my pants.
"See what you have done." I said as I grabbed the counter to get up. Ray was lying on the floor laughing. "What are you laughing for?" I asked him.
"I'm not your uncle at all." He said as he continued to laugh.
"What do you mean?"
"I'm just a billionaire wasting your time." He continued to admit the truth.
"So what is your real name then?" I asked him.
"Jackson." He announced as he pulled out some ID. I looked at it.
"This is a library card from over 20 years ago." I said as I continued to investigate. "This isn't even you." I said to him as he removed his thumb from covering the photo.
"Yes it is." The man said.

"This person has lots of freckles and you don't."
"Well it was over 20 years ago." He said as I thought about it.
"Oh okay, but why would you lie about who you are for 20 years?" I continued.
"Because." He said as he whipped out his wallet. "I'm a millionaire and I don't want anyone to know." He said as he passed me some more money. "Here take this." He said as he gave me a 20 dollar note.
"No please, I can't take your money." I continued. "Just leave me alone, please." I insisted as I was really angry with him.
"But George!" The man said.
"I can't trust you." I continued as he got up and slowly walked out of the fire exit at the back of the store.
"I love you." He suddenly said.
"Just go!" I said. He looked at me as the door then closed behind him. I just sat there confused at everything that was going on. I then walked over to the sink and began to turn it on. I then plugged the plug in. The water was slowly rising as I just looked at the water filling up the sink. "I hate you." I said to myself in the reflection of the water. All of a sudden I dived into the water face first and held my head underneath the water for as long as I possibly could. "1 Elephant." I said to myself under the water trying to drown myself. I held myself under the water for as long as possible. All of a sudden I was grabbed from behind and pulled up from the sink. "What are you doing?" I said as I tried to grab my breath.
"I'm here to help you." He said.
"But I told you to leave."
"So? I do what I want." The man continued. I was laying on the floor, with my face all wet.
"Can you just leave me alone?" I said to the man as I was trying to catch my breath.
"I can't!" He said.
"Why not?" I replied to him.
"Because I care about you." He continued.
"You barely know me." I replied as I pointed to the door.
"Is this really what you want to do, kill yourself and end what was a great life?" The man said.
"I have nothing left to live for." I replied.
"What about your mom?" The man said.
"How do you know about her?"
"Because...." He said as he began to stutter.
"Why are you so nervous? I just asked a simple question." I continued as I sat up.
"Well technically, I slept with your mother back in the 80's." The man admitted. I just sat there in confusion.
"What do you mean?"
"We went to high school together and we ended up together at prom." I was so confused at the man.
"Who are you?" I just kept asking him. He didn't say anything as he then left the building. "No, please!" I shouted as he didn't turn around and just left.
"This is what you wanted." He said as he closed the door. I sat there in silence. It must have been 10 minutes before I decided to get up and walk to the front of the store.

50

"Oh yeah, I still haven't cleaned up this mess." I said to myself as I grabbed the broom and bucket and began to clean up. I was going through each of the sweets containers to make sure all the glass pieces were taken out of it. "Oh, this is going to take forever!" I said to myself as I looked outside the window to see that the sun was starting to go down. "How long have I been here?" I asked myself as I put down the broom and began to walk to the front of the store. I slowly opened the door. "How long has that bus stop been there?" I then asked as I slowly walked over to it. The old woman who was sitting at the bus stop turned around and looked at me.
"This stop has been here for ages." She replied.
"I have never noticed it." I said as the woman looked at me.
"Really? This bus stop is outside your store."
"I guess." I shrugged as I was really confused.
"Are you okay?" The woman asked me.
"Me? I'm fine." I said to the woman as I sat down next to her.
"Well you just look very white in the face."
"I just saw someone who I thought was dead." I said.
"Oh yes, that would be scary." The old woman added.
"Yes it would." I replied.
"So how long have you been waiting for the bus?" I then asked.
"Just a couple of minutes." She said.
"That's cool." I replied as I tried to keep the conversation going. All of a sudden a bus came around the corner.
"Speaking of buses." The old lady said.
"Oh, it's here?" I said as I pulled my head up from the floor.
"Yes!" The old lady bellowed.
"No need to be that excited."
"Oh darling, you don't understand." She said.
"Understand what?" I asked.
"You just don't understand, okay?" The lady said.
"Okay okay." I replied as I worried she would do something stupid. I then got up to get onto the bus as the old lady was suddenly upset. "Why are you upset?" I asked her.
"I only ride on these buses to get away from my house all day."
"Why?" I asked.
"Because I can't afford to put on the heating." She replied. I was shocked.
"Why?"
"I don't get paid anymore." The old lady replied.
"Oh, haven't you got a pension or something?" I asked her.
"No, no." She confessed to me. We got onto the bus as I felt sorry for her.
"Have you tried calling the council or something?" I continued to ask her.
"I can't afford to put the phone on and make calls." She said as I looked at her. She was very upset. I pulled something out of my pocket.
"Here!" I said. "Take this." I continued. The old lady was confused.
"What is this?" She said.
"This is a mobile phone." I explained to her.

"Oh!" She exclaimed.

"And you can have it." I added. She began to break down in tears.

"Oh, why are you so kind to me?" She asked me.

"Because everyone has their ups and downs and we all need to support each other." I said as the bus began to move on.

"Oh wow!" She said as she pulled out her purse. "How much do I owe you?"

"You don't owe me anything." I said to her as she gave me £50.

"Here." She said. "Please take this." She insisted as we sat on the bus.

"Oh thanks." I replied as I took the money and put it in my pocket.

"So where are you heading off to?" She asked me.

"I might just go into town and get a couple of things." I said.

"That sounds cool." She continued as the bus was going down the road. The old lady was going through the phone. "So how do I make calls on this thing?" She asked.

"You just put the numbers in and then you dial it."

"Oh wow!" She said as I showed her how to use it. "This is very hard to use." She said as I was confused.

"This is very easy to use, here, give it a go." I said as I passed her the phone.

"Oh, who should I call?" She said as she began to panic.

"Call the council and ask for help about your money." I said.

"I don't know the number." She said as she was getting stressed.

"Hey don't get upset." I said to her as I gave her the number. "Here, I found it on the internet."

"What's the internet?" She asked as the bus then stopped at her stop.

"It's okay, I will explain it to you later." I said as she slowly walked off the bus with her head still looking at the phone.

"Mind where you are going!" One of the ladies said as she bumped into them.

"Sorry, I'm just discovering this phone thing." She said to the other woman. I looked up to see the commotion. I then sprung up and walked up behind the lady.

"Sorry ma'am." I said to her.

"Keep your grandma in check." She rebutted.

"She ain't my grandma." I told the lady as she then spat at me. I was shocked as the germs went into my eyes. All of a sudden she punched me as the bus came to a screeching halt. Everyone went flying as I tried to hold onto the bus rails. I went forward as I hit my head on the bar above.

15

The bus driver stopped the bus as a car came out of nowhere. "What are you doing?" He shouted to the driver as the passengers on the bus were all injured and hurt. "Does anyone need medical assistance?" The driver then asked.
"Yes!" Several passengers said. As I was still laying on the floor as my head was ringing. The old lady said.
"Hey, can I call the medics?" She said, showing off her new phone.
"I guess?" The driver said as she then began to struggle to dial it.
"Hurry up!" I said as all of a sudden I saw blood coming down from the stairs of the upper deck of the bus. "Hey, there is blood upstairs." I said to the driver as he then grabbed some tissues from his pocket and rushed upstairs. Then unexpectedly there was a loud scream as his body then came falling down the stairs.
"DON'T COME UP!" Someone shouted as they then did a manic laugh. I was shocked and confused as they came downstairs slowly and laughed once more. "Anyone gets off this bus and this thing explodes." He said holding a big red button. Everyone was shocked.
"No please!" I said as the old lady was shocked and scared.
"I have a family."
"I don't care!" The villain said as he grabbed her.
"Hey, let her go!" I said as I got up in a rage and rushed towards him. All of a sudden the button was pushed as the bus began to go up in flames. I dashed out the door as I grabbed the old lady and the villain and we all jumped off the bus. We all landed on the floor as I was up against something sharp. I then reached into his pocket and found a knife. "What is this?" I said to him as I was trying to shield my face from the explosion.
"Hey, give me back my knife." The villain said as his mask then fell off.
"You!" I said as I was shocked. "What are you doing here?!"
"You know this guy?" The old lady said.
"Yes!" I replied. "We spent some time in prison together." I said. "I thought you died dude."
"Not a chance." Billy replied.
"But why are you here? Why did you blow up the bus." I asked him.
"Because you didn't complete your tasks for me." He explained.
"But I thought you died."
"First rule of anything is never suspect that I died." I rolled my eyes.
"Am I in trouble?" I asked him as the police began to come to the scene. Billy then grabbed me and the old lady as we dashed far away from the scene.
"Where are we going?" The old lady said as she was upset. "I need to go home." She suddenly added.
"Not a chance, you are with me now." Billy said as he continued to laugh.
"Please Billy, take me and let the old lady go." I said as I looked at her. The police were beginning to surround the area.
"You don't even know her name, do you?" Billy said to me.

"Look, that isn't important." I said as we went down a small pathway. A car then began to pull up. "What's going on?" I said as the old lady and I were shoved into the back of the car. The old lady screamed at the top of her lungs.
"Please stop, my heart can't take all of this." She said as we were cramped into the car.
"Sorry about this." I said to the old lady.
"Don't be sorry." She said to me. "This thing used to happen to me all the time." She said. I looked confused.
"What do you mean?" I asked her.
"I used to be in the secret service." She admitted as she reached into her pocket and pulled out her badge. I was stunned.
"Why didn't you say anything?"
"Because I had my memory wiped." She confessed as Billy got into the front of the car and put the car into drive.
"So, are you pretending you don't know how to use a mobile phone?" I asked her.
"Yes!" She replied as Billy turned around and said.
"Shut up! Shut UP!" He continued over and over as he then drove away from the burning bus.
"What are you going to do to us now, that you ain't going to do in the future?" I asked him as I began to get angry with him.
"Okay okay, just keep it down, okay." He said as he had a change of heart. The old lady showed me her badge.
"Oh. Your name is Doris?" I said as I was reading it. "My grandmother's name was also named Doris." I said as I looked her in the eyes. She winked as Billy was driving like a maniac. "Where are we going?" I asked Billy.
"You will find out soon." He said as he closed the shutter between the front and the back of the car. I continued to ask Doris some questions about the time in the secret service.
"Oh wow!" I said as she was spilling a lot of secrets. "How can you remember all of this but not how to use a phone?" I asked her.
"I don't know." She said as all of a sudden Billy stopped the car dead in the tracks.
"What's going on?" I said as suddenly the doors opened.
"Get out!" He demanded as he pointed his knife at me.
"Okay okay." I said as I didn't want to get hurt. "I'll do whatever you want Billy, but please, just stop the threats. I can't take it anymore." Billy looked at me as he then moved the knife closer to my neck.
"Don't think I won't do it." He said to me.
"Do it then!" I said as I began to get depressed with everything that was happening. All of a sudden there was a loud whack sound as Doris hit Billy over the head with a brick.
"There!" She said as she smiled at me. "You are free as a bird." She continued as Billy was laying on the floor.
"But why did you do that?" I asked Doris.
"Because you deserve better." She said as all of a sudden Billy grabbed Doris' foot. She went tumbling down to the ground.
"DORIS!" I screamed as I stepped on Billy's hand trying to stop him from attacking her but he wouldn't stop. "Stop!" I said as I picked up the brick and continued to smash it into his head. "I hate you." I said with a passion as he wouldn't stop. "DIE, BEAST!" I said as I finally put the

brick right through his skull. His eye popped out of the socket as there was so much blood. Doris grabbed me and pulled me back.

"I understand that you are upset, but this is just unacceptable." Doris said as I looked at my hands as they were covered in blood.

"Did I really do this?" I asked myself as I saw Billy's damaged face lying there on the ground.

"No, this isn't me." I said as I turned around and hugged Doris. "I'm sorry." I said to her.

"It's not me, you have to say sorry too." She said as she got back into the car. "Let's get out of here." She said as she tried to start the engine of the car.

"Okay." I said as I got in the back seat waiting for Doris to start up the car. Doris then put her foot on the gas as it sped off, leaving Billy to lie on the pavement, bleeding.

"Did we really just do that?" I asked Doris.

"Look, I know it was hard but it had to be done." She said as she then put on her shades. She was speeding down the highway as I was holding onto the back of the seat.

"Can you slow down?" I asked her as she took a sharp turn. All of a sudden we came to a screeching halt.

"Here we are!" Doris announced as we stopped outside of a library.

"What are we doing here?" I asked her.

"You know." She said as she tapped her nose.

"No, I don't, that's why I'm asking." I said as Doris turned around.

"Why don't we go in and find out!" She said as she kept winking at me.

"I don't know what you are winking at." I said as I was really confused.

"Get out and I will show you." She continued as I got out the back of the car and began to walk into the library. We entered through the front door.

"Oh Doris, you are back and who is your friend?" The person behind the desk said.

"This is George." Doris said as I just kept silent and followed Doris around. We walked to the back of the library. The lady then pulled one of the books down as it opened a secret doorway.

"Wow!" I said as I was shocked. Doris then went in first.

"What are you waiting for?" She said as I was just in shock at everything that was happening.

"Where are we going?" I asked Doris.

"You'll find out." She said as she then opened the door to a secret headquarters.

"What is this place?" I asked as I stood there in confusion watching everyone in motion.

"This is the secret service place I was telling you about." Doris replied as she introduced me to her daughter. "This is my daughter, Jasmine." Doris said.

"Nice to meet you" Jasmine said.

"So, what am I doing here?" I asked her.

"Well I think you would make a good member of the secret service." Doris said as Jasmine nodded her head.

"But...." I said in confusion. "I don't want to go on secret missions doing stuff for the government."

"Everyone says that the first time." Jasmine said as she was writing stuff down. I looked at Jasmine then I looked back at Doris.

"Okay, I'll give it a go!" I said in confidence as Jasmine handed me a security badge.

"Use this to get around the headquarters." She said.

"I'm sure my daughter will keep you in good hands." Doris said as she sat down and had a cup of coffee.
"So what do we do around here?" I asked Jasmine.
"Well let me show you." She said as we walked down some stairs as she then opened up a door with her secret pass. The door slowly opened as I began to get nervous. "Well, we keep the first job nice and simple." Jasmine said.
"Oh, I'm not into paper copying and writing stuff down." I said.
"It's not that." She replied as I then looked up and saw the team cracking on with their tasks as I looked over the wall of computers.
"Hey Jas." A man said as he came over and patted Jas on the butt.
"Hey baby." Jasmine replied to him as she kissed him on the lips. Suddenly I felt something inside of me. "This is Paddy." Jasmine said as they were holding hands.
"Nice to meet you." I said as I shook his hand. All of a sudden I was getting sweaty.
"This new guy is here to work with us." Jasmine said as Paddy nodded his head.
"Oh that's great, we could use a set of extra hands." Paddy continued to say.
"What do I need to do, chief?" I asked Paddy.
"Well could you do some art for us?" He said.
"Oh okay, I'm very good at microsoft paint." I replied. Paddy looked at me in confusion.
"Don't you do anything else?" Paddy asked me as we both sat down as Jasmine was walking away.
"I'm not really tech savvy." I said as Paddy opened up the computer and opened up photoshop and began to show me how to use the computer. "So how did you and Jasmine meet?" I suddenly asked as he was showing me through the program.
"Oh we met here." Paddy said.
"She is very pretty and I wish the best for you two." I said to Paddy.
"Thank you man." Paddy replied as I was getting nervous around him.
"I think I might have a crush on Jasmine." I said to myself under my breath. Paddy continued to show me how to work the program for the next 10 minutes. "Oh wow." I said. "How much do I get paid?" I suddenly blurted out.
"Well that depends on your performance." Paddy replied.
"Oh." I said as I then got up and looked at Paddy. "If I don't get paid then I'm not doing it." I said.
"Don't start acting like a child." Paddy replied as he was sipping on his coffee.
"I'm not acting like a child." I said as the rest of the company turned around and looked at us fighting. Paddy then took a big breath in.
"Look, I don't have time for children." He said as he turned away and marched back to his desk.
"I'm just asking how much I get paid." I said. "Simple question." I continued as Paddy was ignoring me.
"Look, isn't working for the secret service enough." He said as he smirked. I was so confused.
"No?" I replied. "I have to feed myself." I continued.
"You can get all the food you want here." He said as he suddenly showed me some sort of food pass. I rushed over and looked at it.
"I didn't know about this."
"It's just one of the many perks you get here." Paddy added.

"Oh okay." I replied. "I'm sorry." I continued as I grabbed his card and rushed into the lunch hall as I hadn't eaten in a long time. I rushed into the hall and bumped into Jasmine. "Oh you!" I said as she was brushing off the crumbs from her dress as she was eating some sausage rolls. She turned around with a face full of sausage.
"Hello, George." She said. "What are you doing here?" She said as she was surprised.
"I'm just getting some lunch." I said.
"But who let you in here?" She asked.
"Your husband!" I explained as I showed her the card.
"Oh, he knows he shouldn't be giving that out to everyone." Jasmine said as I just stood there in awe at her.
"You have very nice eyes." I said to her.
"Oh thank you." She said as she suddenly blushed.
"Do you want to get a coffee with me?" I suddenly asked, making myself look like an ass.
"I'm sorry, A) I'm married and B) I'm busy." Jasmine said as I felt like a right idiot.
"What do you see in that idiot?" I asked her. She was confused.
"Paddy?" She replied.
"Yes." I replied to her.
"He is so kind and handsome." I laughed as she blurted out rubbish.
"Just spending half an hour with him was horrible."
"Why?" Jasmine asked.
"Something just felt off with him." I said to Jasmine as all of a sudden I grabbed her hand.
"What are you doing?" She said to me.
"I feel you are making a mistake." I said to her as she was shocked.
"Excuse me, you know me for 10 minutes, you don't know my life story." Jasmine said as she tried to get her hand out of my hand. "Let go!" She said as she suddenly did a surprise takedown on me. I fell to the floor as she was standing over me like a titan. "Are you going to let go now?" She asked.
"Not a chance." I said as I was smiling, holding onto her hand. "I bet you like it."
"Like what?" Jasmine said as all the other staff were watching. "I'm in love with Paddy, I always have and I always will." She said as she let go of my hand.
"You are lying." I said cheekily. She then slapped me.
"Don't you ever talk to me like that again." She said as she got angry. She then stepped on my neck as I began to struggle to breathe. I pushed her off. "My office!" She said.
"Which is where?" I asked her. She pointed at her office as I got up and slowly walked towards it. "I'm sorry."
"I don't want to hear it." Jasmine replied as I opened the door to her office. Doris was just sitting there.
"What are you doing here?" I asked her.
"Well not only is Jasmine my daughter, but I also run this place." She said. I was shocked.
"Why didn't you tell me anything about this?" I asked her.
"Because it's a secret?" Doris snapped back as she stood up and walked over to me. I sat down on the chair located next to the desk as I couldn't believe what was going on.
"This has got to be a wind up." I said to myself as Jasmine walked in.
"What do you think you are playing at?" She said loudly as she was clearly angry at me.

"I'm sorry, I'm sorry." I said to her. "I wasn't thinking straight." I continued.
"Well I don't care." Jasmine replied as Doris then said.
"Give him a second chance."
"I can't mother, he has already caused so much chaos today and we have lost $2 million dollars."
"We are not in it for the money." Doris continued to fight for me as Jasmine then pulled out her red book.
"Look how much this place has lost in the last 3 months." Jasmine said.
"We are not in it for the money, we are here to save the world." Doris said as she slammed on the desk.
"How is anyone saving the world by creating stupid logos?" I said as I stood up and looked at the red book.
"You are only losing money because of the amount of expenses you had."
"We need those." Jasmine said as I pointed it out.
"That logo stuff is only training until we get you onto the search team." Doris said.
"Look, we need that ice hockey table." Jasmine replied as both ladies were getting into my head.
"Please just one at a time." I said as I was cracking under the pressure. Suddenly I snapped.
"SHUT UP!" I shouted as both Doris and Jasmine looked at me. I dashed towards Jasmine and slammed her head into the book. "You are just a minx and you should be ashamed of yourself." I said as I kept slamming her head over and over on the book. Doris dashed around the table as she then grabbed me.
"Stop that!"
"Don't tell me what to do." I said to her as I pushed her up against the wall. "You are just an old slut, who is a phony." Doris then did a top secret martial art move as she ducked and got out of me holding her against the wall.
"Not a chance." She said as she pulled out her radio and called for assistance. "We need help in Jasmine's office." She radio called as I was dealing with the rage that consumed my body.
"Put that radio down!" I demanded as I looked at Jasmine as she laid there as loads and loads of blood dripped out of her head. I jumped at Doris as she dodged out of the way again.
"George, you are messing with a black belt in karate."
"Don't you think I know that." I said as I jumped on her as she swung me around. I was thrown against the wall as several officers then rushed in and assisted Doris. They all jumped on me.
"Shut up!" One of them said as they placed handcuffs on me.
"I haven't done anything wrong." I tried to say as they placed tape over my mouth. They stood me up. I tried to speak but the tape was getting all over my mouth. I tried kicking the men, who were very strong looking.
"This will be the last time you try a stunt like this." Doris said. She ripped the tape off my mouth as it felt alot like waxing.
"OW!" I let out as I then spat at her. "You think you are so tough but no one is tougher than me." I said as Doris laughed.
"So you are finally showing your true colors?" She continued, "I knew you were trouble ever since we met." She added as the men then placed more tape over my mouth. "Send him to the cells." Doris said as men were attending to Jasmine as she was still bleeding out all over the

place. I was then escorted out of the office as Doris was trying to tend to her daughter. "Is she going to be okay?" She asked the medics.
"We are doing everything we can." They said to Doris as she grabbed Jasmine's hand.
"Everything is going to be okay darling." She said to her. I was being escorted down the hallway and to the prison cells.
"You guys are making a huge mistake." I said as I bit off the tape from across my mouth. The big strong heavy man then placed the tape across my mouth again.
"Just shut up!" The guard repeated as we were walking through the long maze of hallways. After what felt like 10 minutes of torture. One of the guards opened up the cell door as the other ripped off the tape from my mouth. "Okay, you idiot, you are going to be spending the rest of your time here." The guard said as he kicked me in.
"I haven't done anything wrong." I said, trying to bend the bars.
"Here's your food." One of the other guards said as they threw a hamburger at me.
"I'm vegan." I suddenly said, trying to confuse them.
"I don't care." The guards said together as they closed the cell door and locked it up. I began to look around the cell trying to find a way out.
"I shouldn't be in here." I said as I sat down on the bed. All of a sudden I felt the bed collapse underneath me. "Ow!" I said as I got up and lifted up the bed. I picked up the planks of wood that had been broken in half and pulled them all out, leaving the mattress to slide down into the hole between the two walls. I then sat on the mattress as I was playing around with the pieces of wood. "I wonder if I can use these for something?" I said as I looked at the window high above on the wall. "I wonder if I can build a ladder?" I muttered under my breath as I didn't want the guards hearing me. "Excuse me!" I suddenly asked the guard that was standing watching the cells. "How is Jasmine doing?" The guard was shocked.
"Like you care." He said.
"I do." I replied.
"If you cared you wouldn't have hit her." The guard said.
"It was a moment of madness." I repeated as the guards looked at me.
"I don't care." The guard said as he then pulled down the shutters. "Go to sleep." He said as he then turned around and didn't watch me anymore. I then began creating a ladder with the pieces of wood. I then slowly climbed the ladder as I didn't want to break it and make a noise and wake the guards. I reached the window on the wobbly ladder I had created.

16

All of a sudden the wooden planks gave way as everything fell to the ground. I grabbed onto the bars of the windows as I was hovering over my bed. "I can do this." I said to myself as I managed to pull myself up to the window and started attacking the cell bars. I looked down as the guards heard the noise and came rushing in.

"HEY!" One of them shouted. I then spat at them as I managed to pull off one of the cell bars and I then slid into the air vents where the window was connected two.

"So long suckers!" I said as I turned around and went on with my mission. The guards were radioing for more backup.

"He has gone up in the air vents." One of them said as they began to start throwing the wood pallets at me. I started going through the air vents as I was trying to find a way out where I wouldn't be caught out by the guards. I must have crawled around for over 20 minutes as the alarm was going over and over in my ear. All of a sudden I turned a right corner as I looked around and saw an opening. I went over to the opening and looked through it. All I saw was Jasmine laying in the medical bed. I then began to tear up as I looked at her.

"This is all my fault." I said to myself as I felt guilty. Jasmine then flat lined. I was shocked. I didn't know what to do. She was shaking up and down. "I have to do something." I said as no one was even close to helping her. I then rattled the cell bars as I tried to get in there. I suddenly shouted. "SOMEONE HELP!" No one was listening. I then ripped off the bars as I needed to get down there and perform CPR. "Come on, come on!" I said to myself as the bars were slowly moving. I kicked down on the bars as one of them slowly broke. I tried to squeeze myself through the tiny gap. The other bar then broke off. I then landed on my feet as Jasmine was still flat lining. "I'm here." I said as I tried to perform CPR on her. "Come on!" I said as I didn't want her to die. "I love you." I suddenly said as her eyes began to open. She gazed at me. "Yes!" I said as I pumped my fist in the air as I somehow made her survive. "I love you." I suddenly said again. She began to frown.

"Oh, it's you." She said as she began talking.

"I just saved your life." I said to her.

"Well you are the one to put me in here." She replied, showing off her bruises from the attack.

"I'm sorry once again." I said. "That was a mistake, I was angry at you and your mother and I shouldn't have hurt you." I continued to say as I got down on one knee. "I really really like you Jasmine." I said to her as I grabbed her hand. She pulled her hand away as all of a sudden I heard a knock at the door.

"What's going on in there?" Someone said as they tried to open the door. "It's locked." He said to himself as I turned around and began to look for stuff to block up the door. I took the cupboard and blocked the door with it.

"What are you doing?" Jasmine asked as I was pushing the cupboard with all my might.

"I can't let them in here." I said to her.

"But I need medical attention." She said.

"I know and I'm here." I said as I was tearing up. "I have never liked anyone before." I said to Jasmine as I walked back over and grabbed her hand.
"I'm with someone." Jasmine insisted.
"He doesn't matter anymore." I said as I then tried to kiss her. She couldn't do anything as she was too ill to move. So I kissed her on the lips.
"What are you doing?" She said to me.
"I love you." I said as she couldn't do anything.
"George, this is borderline rape." She said.
"No it isn't." I replied defending my actions. I then got on top of her.
"Please stop." Jasmine said as she couldn't move her arms or legs. I then began to unzip my pants as Jasmine was shocked. "No, please!" She said as I then began to pull off her clothes. The guards were banging on the door.
"STOP!" One of them shouted as I then proceeded to have sex with Jasmine without her permission.
"You are going to be in so much trouble." She said.
"No one is going to believe you." I said as I then pulled out of her and did my pants up. "That was nice." I said to her.
"No it wasn't." She replied as she began to tear up. She didn't want to look at me. All of a sudden the cupboard fell to the ground as the guards had the strength to bash in.
"Stop right there!" One of them said as I turned around and looked at them.
"Or what?" I questioned as I was still on top of Jasmine. One of the guards then leaped at me as they jumped on the bed. Jasmine was underneath as she couldn't feel a thing.
"Please get off me." She said as I then jumped down as the other guard then grabbed me. All of a sudden Jasmine then suffered a heart attack. The guards turned around as I managed to then dash out of the room as they tried to help Jasmine. I then ran down the hallway and slid into a cupboard as I needed to get the guards off my back.
"This place is too big for me." I said as all of a sudden I leaned against the wall. It began to turn around. "What's going on?" I said as I grabbed the wall as I was then transported to an office room. "Oh wow!" I said in surprise as I jumped off the turntable and began to look around the office. "Why would they have that secret pathway in this huge place?" I said to myself as I sat on a chair and began to lean back. All of a sudden the alarm began to go off. I fell to the floor as I then hit my head on the ground. "Ow!" I said as I was laying on the floor looking at the ceiling. I then pointed at a hole in the ceiling. "What's that?" I said as I slowly got myself up and began to try to get up to the hole in the ceiling. I then began to crawl around the air vents as I really wanted to see where this room led to. I turned to the left at a T junction as all of a sudden the smell began to pick up. "What's that smell?" I asked myself as I continued to crawl across the air vents. The smell was picking up with each step I took. "What the fuck." I said to myself as I looked down and spotted a body laying on the floor.
"Is that what I think it is?" I said to myself as I tried to open the vent. I jumped down and landed next to the body. I turned the body over as I was covering my nose as the smell was uncontrollable. "You!" I said as I saw the face. I was shocked. "Dad!" I said as I turned it over completely and laid the body on his back. "I haven't seen you for years." I said to the lifeless body. "How did you get here?" I asked him as there was no reply. "I thought you died so many

years ago." I continued to say. "My mom was upset like you've never seen her before." All of a sudden the door behind me opened.
"Excuse me." The man said. "What are you doing here?" The man continued as he brought in his bucket and mop. "This place is off limits." He added as I got up.
"What have you done to my dad?" I said to him.
"I don't know anything about that." The man said.
"Then why are you coming in here?" I asked him.
"I just have to do what the boss says." He replied.
"How long has my dad been here?" I continued to ask him.
"At least the 3 months I've been here." He said.
"And have you told anyone?" I kept questioning him.
"Yes, I questioned it on my first day." The man said as he closed the door.
"And you just continued with the body just laying here."
"Look, I understand you are angry but I'm only here for a paycheck." The man said. I rolled my eyes as he continued clearing up.
"Okay but if you help me, you can be in for big money."
"I don't need money."
"You just said you were working here for the money."
"I am." The man said as all of a sudden someone else came into the room.
"Hey Bart." The woman said as Bart quietly closed the door and then kissed the woman on the cheek.
"Just a second darling." Bart replied as I was watching him. "So if you could leave us alone, that would be great." He said as he was just about to head into the cupboard.
"But I still have so many questions."
"I don't care." Bart said as he closed the cupboard door. I then began to search through my dad's body as I needed to find clues on how he got here. I went through his right pocket and I found something.
"What's this?" I said to myself as I was shocked as I was then reading a notebook. "I love her." I continued reading. "I love Doris." The notebook said. I was shocked. "Doris isn't my mother, was my dad having an affair?" I said to myself as I then went through the rest of the pockets. I then pulled out an ID card. "What's this?" I said to myself as I then turned it over and saw a lot of blood on the other side. "Why is there so much blood here?" I said to myself as Bart and his mistress were getting busy in the cupboard. "My dad was killed and I think I know who killed him." I said as I then pulled out a key from his top pocket. "What is this for?" I said as I pocketed it. I then began to get up and walk around as I needed to find out what happened to my father. I then banged on the door that Bart was getting busy in.
"Not now!" He said to me.
"But I need to tell you something." I said to him. I then waited for a few seconds as his head then popped out of the door.
"What is it?" He said.
"What is this?" I replied as I showed him the ID of my father.
"That's the ID to the higher offices." He said. "Now can I get back to it." He continued.
"Yer I guess." I replied as he then slammed the door quickly as he then continued to get busy. I then walked to the door that Bart came into and tried to pull the handle. All of a sudden it then

fell off. "What?" I said to myself as I then picked it up and tried to plug it in. I then managed to get the door open and I looked around. All of a sudden there were two guards standing next to the door. One of them turned to me and looked up and down.

"Who are you?" He said. I then showed my dad's ID. "Oh sorry sir, carry on." The guard said as I managed to trick him. I then began walking down the hallways wiping the blood off the shoes. I must have walked for over 5 minutes before turning to the door on the left. I knocked on the door.

"Come in!" The man sitting at the desk shouted. I slowly opened the door. "Jack!" The man said as he turned around in his chair. "I have been expecting you." He continued as he then looked at me. "Who are you?" The man said.

"I'm not Jack." I replied as I was certain I wasn't Jack.

"I can see that." The man replied as he then reached for the guard button. I then dashed across the room and stopped him from pressing the button. "What are you doing?" The man said as I was grabbing his arm. "Let go." The man continued as I didn't say a word.

"No!" I then said as I spat at him.

"HEY!" The man yelled. "Guards!" He added as I then put my other hand over his mouth. "Shut up!" He tried biting my hand as I then said.

"I'm here to find out what happened to my father."

"I don't even know who you are." The man said as I took my hand off his mouth and reached into my pocket for my dad's ID. I then showed him it. "Oh wow!" The man said. "I haven't seen that ID in years." He continued.

"Tell me what happened to him." I said as I then sat down on the chair.

"Look, you have to understand that it was a mistake and everyday that goes by, I miss him."

"Not as much as I miss him." I replied.

"I understand." The man said. "Look it was a cool dark night and we had agents go into this top secret base to stop the enemy and we just tried our best to stop him, but we couldn't and unfortunately your father was a casualty of that mission." The man said.

"But why is his body in an office and the janitor just ignoring it."

"Look, we had to keep the body for legal reasons." The man said.

"What reasons?" I said as I banged on the desk.

"I can't disclose them." He said. I looked at him.

"What do you mean?" I said.

"I can't tell you why we had to keep the body." I then grabbed him.

"You will tell me." I said as I was threatening him.

"Look son, we have special rules around these parts and we just can't go around telling them to any old joe." The man said. I then looked at the photos on his desk. I then pointed at them.

"So what would happen if anything happened to your wife or daughter?" I asked him.

"I would be upset like there was no tomorrow." The man said.

"And that's what I am feeling now." I explained.

"Look, look!" The man said as he then grabbed the piece of paper and began to write stuff down. "Here." The man said as he gave me the piece of paper.

"What is this?" I asked the man.

"This is who you need to talk to if you need answers." The man continued.

"But why can't I get them from you?" I asked.

"Because I have nothing to add." The man said as he then pushed me away. "Now get out of my office." He said as I took the piece of paper and put it in my pocket.
"You are lucky, Mr. Brown." I said as I looked at the name sign on his desk.
"That isn't even my name." Mr. Brown said.
"Then what is it?"
"None of your business." He said as he then pointed me out of the office.
"Okay okay." I said to him. I then left the room. I then felt my pockets. "OH SHIT!" I said to myself as I turned around and looked through the window. I then spotted the man take the ID of my dad and put it in the shredder. I began banging on the door. "What are you doing?" I shouted at him as all of a sudden a guard turned the corner of the hallway.
"What are you doing?" The guard asked me.
"You should be asking him that." I said as I pointed to the man inside the office.
"What about Mr. B. Rown?" The guard asked.
"He stole my Dad's ID." I said to him,
"I don't care, where is your ID?" He asked me. I then began to sweat.
"I don't have one." I then said to him.
"What do you mean?" The guard asked as he got inpatient. "Look, you need an ID otherwise you will be taken outside." The guard continued.
"I am just here to take a tour around this place." I then said.
"Oh, then you are going to have to go out until we get your full name and address."
"But what about my dad's ID?"
"I will inform him about that later." The guard said as I then showed him the piece of paper.
"I really need to talk to this guy." I said as the guard grabbed me and then began to escort me out.
"You can call him or something." The guard said as he then pushed me further down the hallway.
"Please." I pleaded with him.
"I can't." The guard continued as I then dropped the piece of paper on the floor as he then closed the door behind me. I then walked over to the bench opposite the HQ. I then sat down and began to cry.
"This is all my fault." I said to myself as it began to rain. "Oh great!" I said as all my luck was unfolding. Suddenly one of the legs of the bench then collapsed. "Ow!" I said to myself as I hit the ground. "I just can't believe it." I said as all of a sudden the guard came back out and said to me.
"Hey dude, you forgot this." He said as he passed me the remains of the ID of my dad. I then smiled.
"Oh thank you." I said as the guard also gave me a banana.
"Here, in case you are hungry." He said as I smiled.
"Thank you." I replied as he came and sat down next to me.
"I'm sorry to hear about your dad by the way." The guard said. "My father wasn't much in my life and it hurts everyday not knowing who he was or why he left."
"Oh I'm sorry to hear that." I said to the guard as he began tearing up. "Do you want a bit of my banana?" I asked him.

"No, no." I'm fine. The guard continued as he then cried. I then proceeded to hug him. All of a sudden he pulled back from the hugging and looked me in the eye. He then kissed me.
"What are you doing?" I said as I pushed him away.
"Sorry, I thought it's what you wanted." The guard said.
"I don't even know your name." I said to him.
"It's Jack." He said as he showed me his ID badge.
"Oh I used to know a different Jack in primary school." I said to him.
"Oh cool." Jack said.
"He used to get in trouble for everything." I continued.
"Same." Jack replied.
"I think one time he got in trouble for blocking the toilets."
"No way, I used to do that." Jack continued.
"Oh." I suddenly realized as I then said. "You didn't go to Hill Valley High?" I asked him.
"Why yes I did." Jack replied.
"Oh." I said once more. "So did I." I continued as Jack said.
"I knew I recognized that beautiful face." He said to me as he then tried to kiss me again. I pushed him away.
"Dude, I'm not gay." I said as he then got angry.
"I used to like you, and I put secret messages in your locker."
"Those were from you?" I said as I was confused. "I thought they were from Jesse."
"Jesse wouldn't go out with you in 100 years." Jack said as I then finished eating the banana.
"Oh." I repeated as all of a sudden there was a car that pulled up next to us.
"Jack!" The driver said.
"This is my ride." Jack said as he got up and walked over to the car. I looked at him.
"Can I come with you?" I asked Jack. He turned around and smiled.
"Of course!" Jack said as he opened the door for me to get into the car.
"So where are we going?" I asked Jack.
"We are going to a strip club." Jack replied.
"Oh!" I said surprised. "Is this what you normally do?" I asked him.
"What do you mean?" He replied.
"Just get off work and then go straight to the strip club." I said.
"Well I have nowhere else to go." He said as I closed the door.
"What do you mean by that?" I asked him.
"Well my husband left me." Jack replied.
"Oh I'm sorry to hear that!" I said as the driver then put the car into drive and began to drive off onto the motorway. "So are you going to the strip club to find a new partner?" I asked.
"Well, who knows what will happen?" Jack said as I then turned away from him to look at the window. I was just sitting there for over 20 minutes as Jack was talking to the driver. I then looked at the strip club as we just turned the corner into it.
"Is this where we are partying?" I asked Jack as the place looked like a shit hole. "Not even my mom would want to work here!" I said as Jack then got out of the car. I was still sitting inside.
"So how will you be paying? Cash or card." The driver said. I then began to get nervous as I didn't have any money. I then looked at Jack as he was walking into the club.

"JACK!" I shouted as he forgot to pay. "I NEED SOME MONEY!" I shouted again. He didn't respond. "Look dude, I don't have any money."
"I don't care." Me and the driver exchanged words. "I need payment otherwise you are not getting out of this car." He said he then locked the car door.
"If you are going to lock me in, how am I going to get you some money?" I said as he then began to put the car into reverse and park the car up. He then got out of the car as he locked me in it. "Sir, you can't do this, it's illegal." I said kicking and screaming trying to get out of the car. Everyone was just looking at me. "Hey sir, over there, come here and open up the car." I said to him. He shook his head.
"I don't want to get involved with your bullshit." He said as he turned away. I continued to push and pull on the door handle as I tried to get the door open.
"Please let me out." I said as the driver was still inside the club. I then push the door much harder. All of a sudden it came off and I fell out of the car and onto the ground. "OW!" I said to myself as I dusted myself off and walked towards the strip club. The bouncer then stood in my way.
"What do you think you are doing?" He asked.
"I need to go see a few people." I said.
"Not a chance." The bouncer said as I tried to get past him anyway.
"I really need to see these people." I said.
"Look, I can't let anyone else in, there is a secret meeting going on." The bouncer replied.
"But I just saw my friend go in there."
"Well he showed me the ID and I let him in."
"He stole my dad's ID." I said.
"I don't care." The bouncer continued.
"You gotta let me in otherwise there will be trouble." I said to the bouncer as he kept pushing me back.
"Oh yeah, what sort of trouble?" He asked.
"They are planning to kill someone."
"I don't care." The bouncer said as all of a sudden I then punched him. He dodged out of the way as I then skid past him and snuck into the door.
"STOP EVERYTHING!" I blurted out as I busted into the room as everyone was talking about whatever they were talking about. Jack then looked at me.
"What are you doing?" Jack said to me.
"I'm stopping this hit." I said.
"We aren't planning a hit on anyone?" Jack said. I then went red in the face.
"But then what are you doing here?" I asked them.
"We are planning a birthday party." Jack said.
"For who?" I asked.
"We can't say." One of the people chimed in.
"Oh, can I help plan the party then?" I said to them as I looked embarrassed. Jack looked around the room.
"Umm…okay?" He replied as he didn't know what to say. I then walked down to the seats as I sat down next to Jack.
"So who are we planning for?" I asked.

"Well it's just a friend of ours." He replied as I looked around the room. I spotted a man on the other side of the table.
"Don't I know you." I suddenly said to the man on the other side of the table.
"I don't think so." He said. Jack then winked at the man.
"What's going on?" I said to Jack.
"Nothing." He said as he tried to not smirk. All of a sudden the man's mustache started to fall off.
"Excuse me." I said as I got up, really confused. "Something is going on here and I need to be told right away." I said as I began to get stressed and began to panic.
"SURPRISE!" Everyone then shouted as they jumped up on the table and balloons and banners fell down from the sky. I was shocked.
"What's going on?" I said as I fell to the floor. The man's mustache fell off as he came over to me and grabbed my hand.
"Brother." He said. I was shocked.
"Who are you?" I asked.
"It's me, your brother." He said.
"I don't have a brother." I replied.
"Well half brother." The man replied. I was in a state of shock.
"But my mom was a saint." I said to him.
"Your dad wasn't." He replied.
"But who is your mom?" I then asked as he reached into his pocket and pulled out a picture of my father and his mother.
"Her?" I said to him
"What about my mother?" The so-called brother said.
"She used to be the local whore." I said.
"So?" He replied.
"I'm just saying." I said to him. "So are we really brothers?" I asked the man.
"Yes!" He said as I stood up and sat down on the chair.
"So what's your name?" I asked him as everyone else was just looking at us.
"We will let you get to know each other." Jack said as everyone else left the room.
"My name is Reg." The man introduced himself.
"Oh Reg, that is a nice name, my name is George." I said to him.
"So tell me more about your mom." I asked Reg.
"Well she wasn't really in my life." He said to me.
"Oh, I'm sorry to hear that." I said to him.
"My mom was always supportive to me and she helped me become the man I am today." I continued as Reg was writing it down.
"Oh okay." Reg replied. "Our dad wasn't really in my life, was he in yours a lot?"
"No not really, actually I found out that he died recently."
"Oh!" Reg said as he was shocked. "I didn't know that, I just assumed he died when I was young." Reg replied. I then pulled out the remains of the ID card and showed him.
"Here." I said to Reg.
"This isn't my dad." Reg replied.
"But this is my dad." I said to him.
"No, he had a different name." Reg replied.

"Oh." I said, shocked. Reg then reached into his pocket and began to search for a picture of his father.
"Here." Reg said as he showed me.
"This is my father, he was just using a different name." I said.
"Oh!" Reg said as he smacked his head. "I can see it now." Reg said as he pointed at his nose. "Oh sorry for doubting you earlier." He said to me.
"No no, it's not a problem." I said to him as he then grabbed my hand. "What are you doing?" I said. He then slowly leaned on me. He then kissed me. I pushed him away. "What the fuck are you doing?" I said as I got up and walked far far away.
"Sorry, I wasn't thinking." Reg said.
"I'm your step brother." I said as I then tried to reach for the door knob. Reg got up and walked up after me.
"No please, you can't tell anyone about this, it was just a mistake." I then opened the door and began to dash out of it. Jack was waiting outside for me.
"How did it go in there?" He asked me.
"Just get me the fuck out of here." I said as Jack then took me back to the car as the driver was waiting inside. "I see you didn't fix the door." I said to the driver.
"What do you expect me to do?" He asked. I shrugged my shoulders. Me and Jack got back into the car as he then started up the engine.
"Can you take us back to my place?" Jack asked.
"Sure." The driver said.
"You haven't even told me your name." I asked the driver.
"My name?" He said. "It's not important."
"So what happened when you and Reg talked?" Jack asked.
"You don't want to know." I replied to Jack as I was holding onto him as I didn't want to fall out of the car as the car door was still open. We must have been driving down the road for over 20 minutes as all of a sudden police sirens came on.
"Oh shit." The driver said.
"What are we going to do?" Jack said as he then began to panic.
"What, why?" I asked as the wind was coming through the gap where the door was as a huge breeze. The driver then put his foot on the brakes. I bashed my head onto the ceiling of the car.
"Ow!" I said as the driver said,
"Sorry!" The police then pulled up behind us.
"What do you think you are doing?" The officer said as he came out of his car and walked up towards us.
"We aren't doing anything illegal, officer." Jack said.
"Well this missing door will say otherwise." The officer replied.
"We are going to get that fixed." The driver said as I was looking at the officer.
"Don't I know you." The officer said to me.
"Me?" I replied. "No no, we have never met before." I continued as I tried to get him off my case. The officer was stroking his beard as he tried to remember me.
"I think I have seen you before." The officer announced as he pulled out a ticket machine. "Do you mind if I take your details?" The officer asked me.
"Umm…sure." I said as I then gave him a fake name.

"Oh okay Jake, just let me run these details through the system." I then laughed as I said to Jack.
"Ha, I lied to an officer." Jack was shaking his head.
"That is very bad George." He said.
"Why?" I replied confused.
"Because now he is going to arrest you for supplying false information."
"But but…" I said as the officer came back.
"That name isn't coming up. How do you spell Wazowski?" The officer asked.
"With two O's." I said as the officer was writing that down.
"Oh okay, let me run that through the computer." The officer said as Jack looked at me disappointed.
"You shouldn't lie to the police officer." He said.
"You do it all the time." I said to him.
"No, I don't!" All of a sudden the driver of the car then got out. The officer dropped everything and rushed over.
"HEY!" He said. "Stop right there." He continued as the driver went round to the trunk. The officer pulled out his gun and was aiming right at him.
"I'm just getting out some bananas." The driver said.
"I don't care." The officer said as then he put his finger on the trigger. "Get back in the car!" He shouted as I was just sitting there in shock.
"Why are you doing this? Because he is black?" I asked the officer. All of a sudden the trigger went off as all I heard was a single bullet. The bullet went straight into the driver's back. He fell to the ground as the officer then radioed for backup. I looked at Jack. "What the fuck." I said as Jack then ducked from the glass that shattered everywhere. The officer then dashed up next to the car, still holding his pistol.
"Now behave." He demanded.
"We haven't done anything." Jack said.
"I don't care." The officer continued to say as the driver was laying at the back of the car, bleeding out of his back.
"Are you going to call an ambulance?" I asked the officer.
"Fuck NO!" He continued to say as he then spat at me. I was shocked.
"HEY!" I yelled at him. "Don't do that to me." I said as I grabbed him and hit him in the nuts. He then dropped the gun as he slowly reached for his balls. I then grabbed the gun and pointed it at him. "Call the medics." I threatened as I was still in the back seat of the car trying to get out.
"No!" The officer replied as he trapped me in the car. "Give me back the gun!" He said to me.
"Not a chance." I repeated as I then tipped all the bullets out of the clip. I then tried to move past the officer as he was still blocking me in the car. I dodged passed him as Jack got out the otherside, we rushed to the driver who was laying on the ground.
"Everything will be okay bro." Jack said as I was shocked.
"He is your brother?" I said to Jack.
"Why yes, where else do you think I am going to get a driver on short notice?" Jack said as he was taking off his top and trying to stop the bleeding. All of a sudden there were two more police cars coming up down the street.
"What are we going to say to the police?" I said to Jack.

"Say the truth?" Jack replied as I was panicking. The officers pulled over and came over to us. "What's going on here?" The officer questioned as he saw the other officer laying on the ground and the gun's bullets all over the floor. "Stay still!" He suddenly said as everyone was panicking. "You shot the officer?" He asked.

"No no, he is just resting after I kicked him in the balls." I admitted as the other officers came over and placed me and Jack in handcuffs.

"We need to get him to a hospital." Jack said as his brother was still laying on the floor.

"Yeah yeah, okay nice prank you are pulling on us." The officer said as they didn't care. Jack's head was slammed against the boot of the police car.

"There is no prank, he has really been shot." Jack said as I was being put in the back of the other police car.

"Please help my friend." I added as the officer got in the front of the car as he then put up the barrier between the front and the back of the police car. The officer then drove off as Jack and his brother were left behind as I looked out the back of the police car. "Please help them!" I said as I was banging on the back of the barrier.

"Sorry, job must be done." The officer replied. I was being transported away from the scene as Jack and his brother were getting no help. I was trying to get out of the car as I was struggling.

"This force is corrupt." I said as the police officer then pulled over the car.

"That is a lie." The officer said as he took out his baton.

"What are you doing?" I said as I then began to get scared. He then turned off the radio as he then walked around to the back of the car. He then began to hit me. "OW!" I said as a bruise came up. He then continued to hit me. I then tried to put myself into a shell as I was trying to protect myself. After 10 long minutes of being beaten up by the police officer. He then walked away. I was wiping the blood from my nose. "What was that for?" I said as I then found one of my teeth on the back seat. The officer then got back into the driving seat as he then turned on his radio. "You are a cunt." I said to him as he then spat at me.

"Fuck you." He said as he continued to get rude at me. I was just trying to regain focus as my head was hurting. He then restarted the car and began to drive off.

"I'm going to tell your bosses." I said to him.

"You won't." The officer said as he then put his foot on the gas.

"Woah! Can you slow down?" I said to him. He looked at me.

"No." He repeated as he then drove around the corner. I hit my head on the ceiling of the car. "Surely this is illegal." I said.

"You will do what I say." The officer continued as I knew I was fighting a losing battle. I then took a big sigh and sat down and looked out the window. All of a sudden the police radio went off.

"All units, all units." They said as I was shocked at what was going on.

"Yes, officer Brown on the way." The officer said as he then drove round the bend. I held onto the handle bar above my head.

"Sir, I need medical assistance." I said as he wasn't listening as he went to the scene of the crime. He didn't say anything. I was still trying to get out of the car as we were flying down the motorway at 100 miles per hour. "Please." I said as I then began to start to feel sick. I banged on the officer's chair. He kept ignoring me. I then threw up on the back seats of the car as I couldn't hold in all the sickness I was feeling. We were driving around town really fast as all of a sudden he slammed on the brakes. I flew forward and slammed my head on the ceiling. The officer then got out of the car. I was banging on the door as I was trying to get out. Everyone was ignoring me as they were dealing with the car crash into the tree. I was looking around the car trying to work my way out. My feet were 10 feet deep in my own vomit and blood as I was trying to look for the key or something. I grabbed the gear stick trying to wiggle it around. It then moved as it went into reverse.

The car suddenly started to go backwards as I was trying to make noise. I couldn't believe what was happening as the car was rolling backwards and slowly going towards the edge of the cliff. I banged on the door once. All of a sudden the car then went over the edge. I screamed as the car plunged into the water. There was a big splash as water began to sneak through the windows as I was just really shocked that this would happen. I tried banging onto the doors, trying to unlock them. "This can't be the end." I said to myself as I then managed to get the door unstuck. It then went flying off. I managed to get out of the car and began to swim for my life. I managed to swim to the surface as I spotted the police officers looking over from the cliff.

"Shit! You let one of our cars go for a swim dude, how are you going to explain that to the chief." One officer said to the other officer.

"I don't know." The officer replied, looking quite embarrassed.

"I'll just say a criminal stole it." He said as the other officer rolled his eyes.

"You are lucky we are friends." The other officer said as I then swam to the end of the stream.

"Quick!" The officer said as I was running out of breath.

"Help me!" I shouted to the police. One of them jumped into the water and began to swim to save me. I was floundering around as I couldn't swim for much longer. All of a sudden someone grabbed my hand.

"Here, come over here." The officer said as the other officer was taking a selfie off the edge of the cliff. "Sorry about that." The officer said as I was being pulled up onto the rocks.

"I'm going to sue your entire force's ass off." I said as I was coughing up water. The officer then pushed me back into the water.

"HEY!" I said as I swam back up to the surface.

"I don't want to help you." He suddenly said.

"You are all the same." I said to him as he was then ignoring me.

"You are going to be in so much trouble." He said to me as he had a change of heart.

"I haven't done anything." I said.

"Well who then controlled the car?" The officer asked. "Because it didn't roll itself down."

"He forgot to put on the brake." I said to him.

"I don't care." The officer said as he jumped into the water and chased me. He then grabbed me.

"What are you doing?" I said as I was trying to swim away. He then put his handcuffs on me.

"No!" I loudly shouted at him as I tried to fight him off. "Go away." I said to him. His gun fell out of his pocket. I then grabbed it. "Don't make me do it." I said as I was then panicking. All of a sudden a gunshot went off. I then looked at my chest as blood began floating up to the surface. I then began to start feeling faint. "You did this!" I said to the officer as I pointed my finger on his chest. He was grabbing me.

"I haven't done anything." The officer said as I then slowly looked up at the sun as I wasn't feeling the best.

"I'm going to die!" I said quietly to him as I grabbed him with all the strength I had left.

"No, you are going to be fine." The officer said as he grabbed me and tried to start swimming to the cliff edge. He placed me on the rocks as he then got up and began to start doing CPR on me.

"It's too late." The other officer said to him as I laid there flat as a pancake. He then kicked the lifeless body. "I can't believe this." The officer said as he began to tear up.

"I didn't mean this to happen. I was just trying to be tough on him."

"I guess you won't be reporting my errors to the boss now." The other officer said.

"What do you mean?" He said.

"Well the whole reason the car fell into the water was my fault." The bad officer said.

"Look, now isn't the time. We need to tell this guy's family."

"I don't care about this guy." The other officer said as he then looked down to the ground. He then reached down and picked up the gun. "Here you go." He said as he then shot the other officer in the back. He went straight down to the ground like a bag of rocks. The officer couldn't believe what he had done. He had gone manic.

"What am I doing?" He said to himself as he looked over at the two lifeless bodies lying up against the river. "I'm going to be in so much trouble." The officer said as he pulled out his wallet and threw all the items on the floor. "I'm going to have to start my life over." The officer admitted as he threw his police radio into the water. He then looked up at the cliff edge as no one was watching him. He then got into the water and began to swim down the stream. He was sweating as he couldn't believe what he had done. "That isn't me." He said to himself as he swam for over 15 minutes as he had now gone on the run. He went over to the riverbank and got out of the water, soaking wet as he dripped water at every step. It was by a road, so the officer waited for a car to come down the road. "I can't believe I did that." He said to himself over and over as suddenly a jeep was coming down the road. The officer stood in the middle of the road as he tried to get the driver's attention. The jeep slowed down as the officer walked up to the driver's window. "Official police business." He said as he showed the driver his uniform.

"Okay, get in!" The driver replied as the police officer walked around to the passengers seat. As he got in, the driver could see he was covered in blood. "Umm…" She muttered. The officer looked at her. "What's with all the blood?" She asked as she pointed at him. The officer then began to get sweaty and was worrying about what to say.

17

"Look, a little accident happened." The officer admitted to the driver as she was shocked.
"I would like you to leave my car now." she demanded. The officer then began to get irate as he then forced himself onto the driver. "Woah! What are you doing?" The driver said as she was scared for her life.
"You are going to enjoy this!" The officer said as he smiled and began to pull out his penis.
"No!" The driver bellowed as the police officer began to start raping her. 10 minutes must have gone by as the officer got off her. "Why did you do that?" The driver asked as she was upset and shocked. The officer didn't say anything.
"Are you going to start this car or what?" The officer questioned as he looked around the car and saw the driver license in the driver's mirror. "Amy, is it?" He asked. Amy didn't know what to say anymore as she was confused at everything.
"Can you just leave my car please?" Amy replied as the officer shook his head. All of a sudden he got out of his side and walked to the driver's side. He pulled Amy out of the car, as she didn't want to put up a fight. The police officer got in the driver's seat as he began to fiddle around with the car. Amy rushed around to the passenger's seat as she didn't want to be stranded in the middle of the desert. All of a sudden the police officer put the jeep into drive and Amy was holding onto the bar as hard as she could as they were flying down the road. "So where are we going?" Amy asked as the police officer was using all the training he had to go down the back roads.
"I don't know." He said.
"I never even caught your name." Amy asked as they were dodging everything in their path.
"My name?" The officer said as he tried to keep calm. "My name isn't important." He said.
"Oh come on, you know my name." Amy replied as she was getting a little mad. The police officer looked at her as he was speeding down the road. "Slow down or the police will catch us." Amy said as she just wanted to get off this wild ride.
"We need to get away." The officer said as all of a sudden he pulled out his gun.
"What are you doing?" Amy asked as he began to point it at her.
"I need to get rid of you." He said.
"No, no!" Amy said as she didn't know what to say. "Dude! You aren't thinking straight." Amy said as she tried to calm him down. The officer then slowed down the car as he then began to break out into tears.
"I can't do this anymore." The officer said.
"Do what?" Amy asked as he was crying.
"I've killed two people." The officer suddenly admitted, Amy was startled.
"Well, I'm sure it was an accident." Amy said as she tried to see the positive side of it. The officer was crying.
"And I raped you." He said.
"Don't worry about it." Amy responded as she didn't want to hurt the officer's feelings. "You are a good person." Amy said as she was trying to be positive. The officer was in a flood of tears.
"My name is Jonathan." He said as he put his hand out to shake it.
"Everything is going to be okay Jonathan." Amy said as she refused to shake his sweaty hand.

"You need to turn yourself in." Amy continued as all of a sudden an unmarked police car pulled up behind the jeep.
"I can't." Jonathan said as he kept shaking his head. Someone then knocked on the driver's door.
"Hello." The undercover police officer said. "You are blocking the road."
"They are here!" Jonathan boasted as he was getting more and more scared.
"It's okay dude, everything will be okay." Amy said as she was trying to calm him down.
Unexpectedly Jonathan put the car into drive and sped off. Amy was shocked as the undercover officer rushed back to the unmarked police car and followed the jeep in pursuit. "What did you do that for?" Amy asked Jonathan as he was focusing on the road. Jonathan was manic as he didn't stop the car. "We need to pull over." Amy said as the car was going a million miles per hour as the police began to chase us. Jonathan didn't say anything as he was looking straight down the road. Amy then all of a sudden grabbed the steering wheel. "Stop the car right now!" She said calmly as Jonathan looked at her. He didn't want to hurt another person. Jonathan let out a big sigh as he began to slow down the car. The car came to a stop as the police began to surround the car.
"Jonathan, come out with your hands up!" The police shouted as Amy slowly exited the jeep.
"I was kidnapped." Amy explained as the police came over and handcuffed her.
"You can say all of that down the station." The officer said as Jonathan tried to get out of the jeep but the officers surrounded him. "You are under arrest for the murders of officer Brown and George."
"George?" Amy said as she overheard the conversation. "George George?" She asked as she had forgotten his surname. The police officer came over and showed her a picture of the dead body. Amy was shaken up as she recognized the man she had an affair with. "Oh yes, that is him." Amy confirmed as the officers wrote it down. Amy was transported into the back of the police car as Jonathan was strip searched. "So what happens now?" Amy asked the officers.
"Well you are going to have to go down the station and answer a couple of questions." The leading officer said as Amy was still in shock that she found out that George had been killed. Amy sat in the back of the police car as she began to get tearful. "I loved him." She said as the officer wasn't listening. The officer then put the car into drive as the car began to start moving away from the scene. "Am I going to get in trouble?" Amy then asked the officer.
"Depends how much you will tell us." The officer replied as Amy was nodding her head.
"I will tell you everything I know, I didn't kill anyone and I was kidnapped." She continued to say as the car was speeding down the motorway. The car then arrived back at the police station where Amy was being taken in for an interview.
"Hello." The officer said as Amy was sitting on the chair opposite. "So tell us everything you know." The officer asked.
"Well I was driving down the road and all of a sudden this guy comes out of the river and runs onto the road, so I stopped as hard as I could and then he just walked into the passenger seat."
"I see…" The officer said as he was taking notes.
"He then got angry at me for not driving so he came around to the other side and chucked me out." Amy said as she was explaining everything.
"So why did you get back into the car?" The officer asked.

"I wasn't going to lose my car, I was going to fight for it." Amy explained. "Wouldn't you want to save your car?" Amy asked.

"Well yes, but I wouldn't get in a car with a lunatic." The officer said as he was just trying to trip Amy up.

"Well, that's your choice." Amy uttered as the officer was still confused.

"You saw the blood on him and yet you went for a ride with him."

"I thought it could be paint." Amy said as she lied to the officer.

"And you go out with most of your friends covered in paint?" The officer spoke.

"I didn't do anything illegal. Charge me or let me go!" Amy demanded as she was getting frustrated with everything.

"Let's settle down." The other officer said as he could see Amy was getting a little enraged.

"Sorry." She said as she didn't know what else to say. "I just want everything to be normal again." Amy continued as she was thinking about George. She began to start tearing up. The officer closest to the wall passed her a dry tissue.

"Here!" He said as she grabbed it and took it to her eyes.

"Thanks." She said.

"Okay, I think we are done here." The officer in charge boasted. Amy got up as she began to walk to the door. "Oh just one more thing." The officer asked. "Why were you dating your nephew?" The officer asked.

"Umm..." Amy stuttered as she became right red. "We didn't know we were related when we met." Amy explained as the officer was suspicious.

"Okay you can go now." He said as Amy opened the door and exited the interview room and left the police station.

"I better see my sister." Amy said to herself as she walked from the police station. Amy walked to the bus stop as she had no other way of getting home. The bus pulled in as Amy tried sneaking on. The bus driver tapped on the glass.

"Excuse me." He said.

"Yes?" Amy responded as she was walking on by.

"Money." The bus driver asked. Amy then blushed as she didn't have any money.

"Umm..." She said as she passed him the tissue she was holding. The bus driver was confused.

"Pay up or get off my bus." He said as Amy then dashed onto the bus as the bus driver opened the door and got out of his cab. "Ma'am, money now or I'm going to get the police involved for fare dodging." The bus driver said as Amy knew she was defeated.

"Okay, okay!" She said as she got off the back of the bus. Amy walked back a few steps as she needed to get her head together. "I suppose I can walk for a bit, it would be good to get a clear head." Amy said as she began walking in the direction of her sister's house. It was a long walk as it was very far away but Amy was enjoying getting in the steps. She continued to smile as the house was just coming up round the corner. Amy then walked up to the front door and knocked on it. "Hello." She said as she waited for someone to open up. "Hello? sis!" She shouted as she was trying to get a response. "I have something to tell you." She continued as no one was answering the door. Amy then looked around as there was no car parked in the driveway. She looked around some more as all of a sudden she spotted the top left window open. "Oh, she doesn't normally have this open." Amy said to herself as she tried to close the window. Without notice she could smell something. "Ew, what's that smell?" She questioned as she tried looking

through the window. She couldn't see anything as out of the blue one of the neighbors came over.
"Are you okay?" She asked.
"I'm just trying to see if my sister is okay." Amy asked as she closed the window.
"Oh no one has been around here for a week." The neighbor explained. "Someone took the car and no one has been seen since." The neighbor continued.
"Oh!" Amy said as she didn't know what to say. "I'm going to call the police." Amy suddenly announced as she tried to think about what to do. The neighbor nodded her head as Amy dialed the police.
"We will send some officers over to your location very shortly." The person down the line said. Amy put the phone down as she waited for the police to arrive. 10 minutes went by as Amy was just playing with her thumbs. The police car then came around the corner as Amy could hear the sirens come closer and closer. The police officer then stepped out of the car.
"Hello." The police officer said as he came closer to Amy.
"Yes, I just want to do a welfare check on my sister." Amy said as she walked over to the door. The police officer then began knocking on the door as no one was responding.
"HELLO!" The officer bellowed as he tried to barge open the door as he couldn't get it open. The other police officer walked around the back of the house as he spotted the window.
"Is this window always open?" The police officer asked.
"I do not know." Amy said as she began to panic.
"Shaun, come here." The officer said as the other police officer came over and gave him a leg up. The police officer squeezed through the window as he landed on the other side.
"What's that smell?" The officer questioned as he got to his feet. Amy and Shaun were waiting outside as the other police officer came and opened the door from the inside. "Here!" He said as he opened up the door. "Let's check all the rooms." The officer said as Shaun followed him in and searched every room. Shaun slowly opened the bedroom door as he then saw something in the mirror.
"In here Dave!" He said in confidence. Dave rushed over. They slowly continued to open the door as they then looked up on the bed as they saw a body hanging from the ceiling.
"Shit!" Dave muttered as he went out to inform Amy. "I'm so sorry." He said as Amy couldn't believe it.
"She wouldn't have killed herself. She had so much to live for." Amy explained.
"Has she gotten into any money problems recently or anything?" Dave then asked.
"I'm not sure, I know she had to take up a second job to cover the losses the sweet shop was losing." Amy admitted.
"Do you think it was taking a lot on her?" Dave then questioned.
"I don't know, she seemed fine with it." Amy said.
"Let's not speculate." Dave continued.
"You are the one asking the questions." Amy replied as Dave then got a little angry.
"Okay." Dave said as he put away his notepad and walked away. Shaun then slowly came over and said
"We need to protect the scene."

"Okay, okay!" Amy said as she was walking away from the house. "I can't believe it." She said to herself as she took a big deep breath in as she tried to focus. She couldn't believe her own sister would take her life. "I thought she was happy." Amy said as Shaun came over.
"Sometimes you think you know someone, but you don't know what they are hiding." He said as he could see Amy was in distress.
"Thanks." Amy replied as she tried to smile. More and more police arrived at the scene.
"Do you have anywhere to spend the night?" Shaun then asked. Amy began to think.
"I don't think so." She replied as Shaun then said.
"You can spend the night at mine." He said as Amy thought about it.
"What about no." Amy replied as Shaun then began to radio around trying to get some answers for Amy.
"What about a hotel room?" Shaun then said.
"Yes yes." Amy said. "But can you give me a lift?" She asked.
"Umm…okay." Shaun said. "Just wait till I'm finished here." He continued as he was continuing to do his policing duties. Amy walked to the edge of the road as the police then took the body out of the house. Amy looked at them, removing the body as she began to tear up.
"I love you." She said as she watched the body being put in the back of the ambulance. She then sat down on the floor as she watched all the police officers do their job. Minutes turned into hours as the sun was setting down as Amy did not move from her spot.
"Are you ready?" Shaun said as he was getting ready to end his shift.
"Okay." Amy said as she got up and smiled.
"Just get into the back of the car and I will be over in a second." Shaun said as he just had a final few things to sort out. 5 more minutes went by as he came to the car. "Okay." Shaun said as he sat in the driver's seat and put the car into motion. "Let's go!" He said as Amy buckled up her seatbelt. The car drove off as Amy looked away from the scene. "I'm so sorry." Shaun began to talk as he was trying to make some conversation.
"It's okay." Amy said as Shaun could see she was upset. It was a long 10 minute ride as Amy didn't really say much.
"Here we are!" Shaun said as they arrived at the hotel after a short journey. "Do you want me to come in with you?" Shaun then said
"Umm…okay." Amy said as she was still upset. Shaun got out of the car and helped Amy out as she was still a little shaken.
"I'm here for you." Shaun said as he was trying to be friendly.
"Thanks." Amy replied as they walked through the hotel doors.
"Hello, this young lady has a room booked by the police." Shaun said as he began to explain everything.
"Okay, that will be room 4A." The hotel receptionist said as she gave Amy the keycard to the room as Shaun then said.
"Are you going to be okay?"
"I don't know." Amy said as she was sad and depressed.
"Let me take you upstairs to make sure that you are okay." The two of them slowly went up the stairs as Amy was getting sadder and sadder.
"I don't think I can do this much longer." Amy then admitted.
"Why?" Shaun said.

"It's just too much." Amy replied as they walked to the hotel room. "What have I got to look forward to, everyone in my family is dead and it's just depressing."
"But remember you are an amazing person."
"I can only hang in there for so long." Amy said as she opened the door to the hotel room and went inside. "Okay you can leave now." Amy said to Shaun.
"Oh okay!" He looked a little disappointed as he really thought Amy was beautiful. Shaun was walking down the hallway as all of a sudden the door reopened.
"Shaun!" Amy shouted at the top of her lungs. Shaun turned around.
"Can you stay with me?" Amy then said as she had a change of heart.
"Okay!" Shaun said as he smiled at her as he rushed over and kissed her. They proceeded to have sex as they slammed the door closed and began to get busy.
"That's just what I needed." Amy said as she got up and smoked a cigar.
"Yes, that was very nice." Shaun said as he was getting his clothes on as he gave Amy a big kiss on the forehead.
"But you do know that was just a one night stand." Amy admitted.
"I suppose." Shaun said as he didn't know what to feel. "It was amazing though." He continued as Amy was looking at him.
"It was a one night stand, nothing more." Amy said as she put her bra on. Shaun got up and put his shirt back on.
"Okay." Shaun said as his phone then began to ring. "I got to take this." He said as he rushed out of the room and took the phone call.
"That was good." Amy said as she felt happier than yesterday. "I know this might be shit right now, but there is always tomorrow." Amy said to herself as she looked around the room to see that Shaun had left his watch on the tableside. "Shit!" She said as she jumped up and rushed out the room. "SHAUN!" She shouted as Shaun was nowhere to be seen. "I better get down the station and return this in." Amy said as she got all her belongings and went downstairs to the hotel's reception. "Here!" Amy said to the receptionist as she handed her back the keycard to the room.
"Thank you!" She replied as she left the hotel and went back to the nearest bus stop. She checked her pockets to make sure she had enough change to get on the bus.
"Okay I got enough." She said as she felt around for the £2 that she needed. The bus then pulled in as Amy then got aboard.
"You!" The bus driver said. "You better have the right money this time or I will not be letting you on." He said as Amy pulled out the money and gave it to him.
"Here you go!" She replied as she went to the top deck of the bus. She went to sit down as all of a sudden her phone then began to ring. "Who could that be?" She said to herself as she sat down at the front. "Hello?" She said down the line. It was an unknown number.
"Hey Amy about last night." The voice said.
"Shaun?" Amy questioned how he got her phone number. "How did you get my number?"
"I put it in while you were sleeping." Shaun replied. "Can we meet up?" He then added as he was a little nervous about talking to her.
"What for?" Amy asked as the bus began to move.
"I just want to see you again."

"I told you yesterday." Amy said as she began to get frustrated with Shaun. "It was just a one night stand, I was feeling lonely and upset, it was just sex nothing else." She began to explain as people started looking at her on the bus.
"Please." Shaun begged as Amy then put down the phone. The phone then immediately rang again as Amy pressed the red button to ignore it. Amy then began to think as she didn't really know where she was going on the bus.
"I suppose I could meet him for a free lunch." Amy then said as she had a change of heart. She began to dial the number as she thought about last night more and more and how she had never had sex like that before. "Shaun." She said as the phone answered. "We can meet for lunch." She continued as Shaun replied.
"Okay okay, I got an hour free a little later."
"We can meet at the little cafe on the corner of Green Street." Amy said as she was looking around on the bus to see who was listening.
"Umm…yeah that would be great." Shaun replied as Amy then put down the phone as she was googling how to get to the cafe.
"Oh yes!" She said to herself as she got up from the bus. She needed to do some walking. She proceeded to get off the bus at the next stop. "Thank you!" She said as she got off and sat at the bus stop for a second to gather her thoughts. "Am I doing the right thing?" She asked herself as out of the blue a car pulled up.
"Need a ride, love?" The driver said. Amy didn't say anything as she was out of it. The driver honked his horn. Amy jumped as she was knocked for six.
"Excuse me?" She said.
"Do you need a ride somewhere?" The driver asked. Amy then thought about it as she needed to get to the cafe but didn't really want to walk.
"Umm…okay." Amy said as she put down her phone and began to enter the car.
"My name is Carl." The driver explained. "So where are we heading?" Carl continued to ask as Amy then said
"Green Street."
"Okay." Carl said as he put the address in the GPS. "So what do you do for a living?" Carl asked as Amy then explained how she was a part time nurse at a local nursing home. "How long have you been doing that?" Carl asked as he was driving down the road.
"Just 7 or so years." Amy explained.
"Do you like doing that?"
"It pays the bills." Amy said as she was watching everything go by. "So do I have to pay for this ride?" Amy then said.
"No no, just being a good human." Carl said as he smiled in the mirror. Amy looked at him with his black teeth and rotten gums.
"So how long have you been a driver?" Amy asked.
"A taxi driver?" Carl replied. "I have never been one." He smiled as Amy then began to freak out.
"What?" Amy said as she was dumbstruck. "Do you just go around picking up people off the street?" She said as she tried to open the door. It was locked. Carl then laughed as they continued to drive down the road. "Let me out you freak!" Amy said as she was kicking the door, trying to open it.
"Please settle down and enjoy the ride." Carl said as he then laughed.

"Who are you working for?" Amy asked.
"What do you mean?" Carl responded.
"Who asked you to get me?"
"No one!" Carl replied as he was dodging traffic and driving crazily down the road. Amy then began to pull out her phone.
"You forgot I have this." Amy boasted as Carl looked at her.
"No!" He belted out as Amy then dialed Shaun's number.
"Hey Shaun." Amy said as Carl then slowed down the car. He stopped the car as he went to the back and pulled the car's backdoor open.
"Give it to me!" Carl said as he was getting angry.
"Go away you creep!" Amy shouted as Carl was getting on top of her.
"No please!" Amy said as she kept kicking him. "Go away!" She shouted louder and louder. Carl then closed the door behind him as he locked it. "What are you doing?" Amy said as Carl was all over her. He smiled as he showed his black teeth once more. Amy didn't say anything as she didn't have the strength anymore as she gave up. Carl then unzipped his pants and began to rape her. Amy held everything in as she began to tear up. 10 minutes had passed as Carl then began to put on his clothes.
"Thanks!" He said.
"Thanks?" Amy replied as she was angry at him. "You just used me like a little playdoll." Amy said as he got up and followed him out the car.
"Get back in the car!" Carl said as he suddenly snapped. "GET BACK IN THE CAR!" He shouted as he was really really angry at Amy.
"No." Amy simply said as she didn't do what she was told. "I'm not your plaything." Amy said as she looked around on the floor. She saw a brick. All of a sudden she picked up the brick and smashed it against Carl's head as he wasn't looking. Carl fell down to the floor as Amy couldn't believe what she had done. All of a sudden the phone rang. Amy picked up the phone as she didn't know who it was.
"Are you okay Amy?" The voice said down the line.
"Umm...yes." Amy replied as she couldn't believe what happened.
"Are you still coming to the cafe?" The voice said.
"Shaun?" She replied.
"I can't, something has come up." She then explained.
"Oh, why did you try to phone me earlier?" Shaun then asked.
"Sorry, that was a butt dial." Amy admitted.
"Oh!" Shaun said as he sounded sad. "It's okay, I know you don't like me." Shaun said. Amy didn't know what to say.
"You are a great friend." Amy said as she didn't want to hurt his feelings.
"Okay." Shaun replied. "Have a great time whatever you are doing?" Shaun said as Amy was panicking.
"Shaun." She suddenly said. "I have done something bad." She continued to explain. Shaun didn't know what to say.
"Okay?" He replied. "And where are you right now?" He then asked.
"I'm at the local gas station." Amy said as the car was in the alleyway behind the gas station.
"Okay okay. I will get over there as soon as possible." Shaun said as Amy was just standing

there as she didn't want to touch the lifeless body. 15 minutes had gone by as Shaun on his bicycle then came up the street. He came to the back of the car.

"What is this?" He said as Amy was just standing there, looking over the body. Shaun then put his bicycle down as he walked towards Amy. "Amy?" He said. Amy didn't say anything as he then saw someone on the floor. "Amy!" He asked again as he grabbed her hand and saw the scene. "Did you do this?" He said as Amy wasn't saying anything.

"It was an accident." Amy suddenly said as Shaun was taken aback.

"I didn't think you had it in you." Shaun said as he saw the brick covered in blood.

"So what are we going to do?" Amy said.

"Umm..." Shaun said as he had to begin thinking about what to do. "We have to move this body somewhere, do you have the keys to the car?" Shaun asked.

"He should have them on him." Amy said as Shaun put on his gloves and began to start feeling around the body.

"Here!" He said as he picked them up. Shaun then threw the keys to Amy as she put the keys in the car engine. "Okay." Shaun said as he began to sweat buckets. "I'm going to need you for this bit." Shaun said as he opened the car door. "I need you to pick up the legs." Shaun said as he began to pick up the torso and used all his strength to move the body. Amy was helping move the lower part of the body as they placed the body in the back of the car.

"Now what?" Amy said as Shaun picked up the brick,

"We are going to need this as well." He said as he put it in the back. "Get in the car as we've got to go now." Shaun said as he was really panicking as he didn't want to get Amy in trouble. Shaun started up the car as Amy got in the passenger seat.

18

"Where are we going?" Amy asked as they drove away.
"What about your bicycle?"
"It's not mine." Shaun said. "An unwanted bike." He continued. "They will never be able to track it back to me." Shaun said as he drove away from the scene.
"Oh okay!" Amy said as she was surprised Shaun knew all of this. "So where are we going?" Amy then asked again as they drove down the road.
"We are going to have to go to the river or something!" Shaun then said.
"Am I going to get in trouble?" Amy then asked.
"No no, we are going to cover this up." Shaun said as he grabbed her hand and said.
"Everything is going to be okay." Amy began to tear up.
"Thanks." She said as Shaun was just focusing on driving the car.
"Can we talk about the other night?" Amy then said as Shaun was listening. "It was good but you aren't really my type." Amy said as Shaun understood.
"It's okay." Shaun said as he let out a big deep breath. "It was my first time in a long while." Shaun said as he smiled at her.
"Oh!" Amy replied as she was shocked. "So how long have you been a police officer?" Amy asked as Shaun said.
"The last 17 years."
"Oh wow! What made you stick with the job for so long?" Amy asked.
"Just that I get to do something different everyday." He continued as he then pulled up to the river bank. "Here!" He said as he stopped the car.
"What are we going to do?" Amy asked.
"We are going to chuck the body and the brick in the river, no one will know." Shaun said as he went to the back door and opened it. He then picked up the brick and tossed it into the river. 'Splash!' It went as it created a little hole. "Okay now for the body." Shaun said as Amy was still sitting in the passenger's seat.
"Okay." Amy said as she got round to the back and picked up the legs of the body.
"Okay on the count of three." Shaun said as they rushed over to the river bank. "One!" He said as they began to start tossing it back and forward. "Two!" Shaun said as Amy was starting to give way as the body was very heavy. "Three!" Shaun said as they threw it into the river, causing a big splash! "Okay that's it!" Shaun said as the body sank to the bottom of the river.
"You mean it?" Amy asked as she didn't know if she would get away with it.
"I have been in this line of work forever, I know what they are looking for." Shaun said as Amy came in for a hug.
"Oh thank you." She said as they embraced each other.
"Don't worry about it." Shaun replied as they looked each other in the eyes.
"You have beautiful blue eyes." Amy said as they looked at each other. All of a sudden Shaun leaned in for a kiss as they kissed for a second time.
"Sorry about that." Shaun said.
"No no, it was nice." Amy replied as they continued to kiss.
"Say we have this jeep all to ourselves." Shaun said as he winked.

"Okay." Amy replied as they headed into the jeep to have sex. The car was rocking back and forth as the river was flowing in the background.
"That was nice." Shaun said as they had finished and laid on the back seats.
"So how was your second time in as many days?" Amy said as she was really happy.
"You make me feel special Amy." Shaun said as he smiled at her.
"So do you." Amy replied as they laid in each other's arms as they were really happy.
"Do you want to go out again?" Shaun asked as he was really nervous.
"Okay." Amy said as she didn't know what to say. They held each other's hand as all of a sudden there was a knock at the car window. "Oh shit!" Amy said as they rushed to get on their clothes as the knock on the window became louder and louder.
"Open up!" The voice said as Amy came out of the car.
"Hello?" She questioned the man who was just looking at them.
"Why have you parked your car here?" The man asked as he was writing stuff down.
"We were just having fun." Amy admitted as Shaun followed Amy out of the car.
"Well you can't park on yellow lines." The traffic warden said.
"Oh." Shaun said as he didn't know. "Sorry, we were just having a little fun." Shaun continued as he pleaded with the traffic warden.
"I'm going to have to issue you with a ticket." He said as he wrote everything down.
"Fine!" Shaun said as he took the ticket.
"You have 14 days to pay it!" He said as Amy then got into the passenger's seat.
"Let's go!" Amy said as the traffic warden walked away. Shaun headed to the driver's seat. "I can't believe that." Amy said as she laughed.
"At least we didn't get caught throwing the body into the river." Shaun said as he turned on the engine.
"So where do you want to go now?" Amy asked.
"I have to get back to work." Shaun said as his phone was ringing.
"Oh okay." Amy said as she didn't know what she was going to do with the rest of her day.
"I'll drop you off at your place." Shaun said as he reversed out of the alleyway. They drove away from the crime scene. 15 minutes went by as Shaun's phone was ringing over and over.
"Are you going to answer that?" Amy asked.
"I can't, I'm driving." Shaun replied as they arrived at Amy's flat. "Here!" He said as he pulled up.
"I'll see you later." He said as Amy got out and walked back to her flat. Shaun then drove away as he picked up his phone.
"Where have you been?" The voice asked as Shaun was watching the road.
"I was out on a job." He said as he lied through his teeth.
"Well we need you back at the station right away." The voice continued as Shaun was driving as fast as he could. He headed back to the station. 12 minutes passed as Shaun then arrived at the station.
"Come on Shaun, we have to get out on the beat." The other police officer said as Shaun parked up the jeep as he dashed out and ran into the locker room to get changed. "I had to cover for you…again!" The man said as he followed Shaun.
"Look Neil, it was just a one off." Shaun said as he was getting changed into his police uniform.
"Well why didn't you answer your phone?" Neil asked as Shaun had got dressed quickly.
"I don't need to answer my phone 24/7." Shaun said as the superintendent came in.

"You two!" He boasted as Neil was looking scared. "I asked you to get out an hour ago."
"Sorry boss, Shaun was just being sick." Neil said as he was lying again.
"Look, I don't care, there is crime being committed and we have to stop them." The superintendent continued as Neil then walked out of the locker room. Shaun followed him as he picked up his hat and they ran to the police car.
"So was it good?" Neil asked as Shaun was embarrassed.
"Don't talk about that." Shaun said as Neil had started the car. "I don't ask about your sex life with your wife." Shaun continued as he was really angry with Neil. "Just go!" Shaun said as he was red in the face. They drove around town as they waited for an incident to respond to. "So how's life?" Shaun asked Neil as all of a sudden they heard,
"Robbery at the local sweet shop." Down the radio line.
"Oh shit!" Neil said as he began to think what was the quickest way to get there. Shaun was holding onto the bar above his head as the car flew down the road. "Hold on!" Neil said as they did a 3 point turn as Shaun was ready. They sped down the road for 5 minutes as they then arrived at the sweet shop to find the window smashed.
"Oh wow!" Shaun said as he got up and began to explore the scene. "Hello!" Shaun shouted as he pulled out his baton and headed in. All of a sudden a shot was heard. "All units, all units!" Shaun said as Neil was still parking the car. "Shots fired, shots fired." Shaun repeated as he headed into the sweet shop. He ducked behind the counter as he heard the rumblings in the back of the shop. Neil then arrived as a gangster then came out from the back.
Go away!" He shouted as Neil stood there with his gun.
"HANDS UP!" He shouted as Shaun began to crawl around the back of the counter to try to attack the gangster without being noticed. All of a sudden the gangster pulled out his gun as he dropped the sack of money.
"You want a fight?" The gangster threatened as he then pulled the trigger. Another shot went off as Shaun covered himself. Shaun then turned around as Neil then dropped to the floor as the gangster then dashed for the exit. "So long suckers!" He said as Shaun rushed over to Neil.
"It's going to be okay." He said as he began to perform CPR on Neil. "Neil, can you hear me?" He said as a person walking by came over to assist.
"I'm a medic, I know CPR." The medic said as she began to perform CPR on Neil. Shaun then radioed for more backup as the scene was descending into chaos. All of a sudden Amy phoned Shaun.
"Shaun." She said as he picked up.
"What is it?" He said as he wasn't in the mood for sex.
"Someone has broken in."
"Where?" He asked.
"The sweet shop."
"I know we are here right now." Shaun said as Amy was relieved.
"Did you stop them?" She then asked.
"No, they took all the money and one of my officers was shot."
"Oh no!" Amy replied. "Do you want me to come down there to lock the shop up?" Amy said.
"Yes if you can." Shaun said as the medic then said.
"Sorry, there is no pulse." The medic continued as Shaun was devastated.
"It's okay." Shaun said as he walked away.

19

More medics and police arrived on the scene as Amy then arrived after 10 minutes. "I'm here!" She said as she rushed over to Shaun. "What's with the glum look?" Amy asked as Shaun was upset.
"We just lost another officer." Shaun said as Amy was shocked.
"Oh!"
"We are running so low on officers these days, we have 1 officer doing the job of 3."
"Why don't I join?" Amy said as she handed the keys to Shaun. "Here are the keys."
"You join the service?" Shaun said as he was delighted. "That is a very good idea." He continued as he took the keys from her.
"So how do I sign up?"
"I will be in touch." Shaun said as he turned around and unlocked the main doors of the sweet shop. Shaun then walked into the back of the sweet shop as he was looking at what was robbed. The forensic team arrived as they began doing their job. Shaun then discovered something as he picked up a picture. It was a picture of Amy and George. Shaun was shocked.
"I thought she liked me." Shaun said as he was disappointed. He took the picture and placed it in his pocket. Shaun walked out of the sweet shop as Amy was still waiting for him.
"Are you okay?" She asked as she could see Shaun was a little rattled.
"Just leave me alone." Shaun said as he was angry.
"What!" Amy said as she was confused.
"You already have a boyfriend." Shaun said as he was upset.
"I don't." Amy said as she was defending herself.
"Then who is this?" Shaun said as he pulled the picture out of his pocket. Amy was surprised as she didn't think she had any pictures of her and George together.
"That's just an ex." Amy said as she was defending her relationship. "He turned out to be my nephew." Shaun was surprised as he was disgusted.
"I thought I knew you." Shaun said as he walked away.
"SHAUN! It was before we met!" Amy shouted as she tried to defend herself and fight for someone she loved.
"Don't bother joining the force because I will veto it." Shaun said as he was angry with her.
"We all have a past, but I want to spend the future with you." Amy suddenly said as she got down on one knee. "Marry me!" She said in a split second. Shaun was dumbfounded as he turned around. He stood still for a minute as he was taking everything in.
"Yes!" He said as he smiled and ran towards Amy. "I love you!" He said with passion as Amy replied
"I love you two, you dumbass." They proceeded to kiss as everyone at the scene clapped as they were happy. "Let's have a shotgun wedding." Amy said as she was desperate to get married to Shaun.
"Umm…okay, once I finish here, we will go down to the wedding office and make it official." Shaun said as he was calling his parents hoping they had nothing planned for the evening. Amy was happy as she smiled as she began walking back to her flat as she needed to get changed into something nice for her big day. Shaun was still on the job, talking to officers and examining

the crime scene. The minutes turned into hours as Shaun then looked at his watch. It was 6pm and time to clock off.
"Okay gang. I'm done here." He said as the other officers wished him good luck at the shotgun wedding.
"I hope it goes well." One of his colleagues chimed in as Shaun walked back to the car he had borrowed from Amy. He got into the car and began to start up the engine as he was getting nervous.
"I can do this." Shaun said to himself as he was trying to get himself ready as he drove away. He drove down the road as he arrived at the wedding office after 20 long minutes of driving. "I'm here." Shaun said as he parked the car and got out. Amy was nowhere to be seen. "I bet she has cold feet." Shaun said as he turned the corner only to see Amy waiting for him.
"Hey babe." Amy said as she was in a stunning blue dress.
"Sorry I didn't have time to change." Shaun replied as he walked up the steps and grabbed Amy's hand.
"It's okay." Amy said. "You are a wonderful person and I want to spend the rest of my life with you." Amy continued as they both walked into the office.
"That would be £100." The receptionist said as Shaun pulled out his wallet and paid the money.
"Okay the pastor will be with you shortly." The receptionist said as she pointed to the room. All of a sudden Shaun's parents turned up.
"SHAUN!" They shouted as Shaun and Amy turned around. "You didn't think you would get married without your mom and dad being there." They said as they came over and gave Shaun a hug.
"Are you sure you want to do this?" Shaun's mother said.
"Yes!" Shaun said nervously as he was scared.
"We will always be behind you." Shaun's dad continued to say as Amy was ready to get married.
"Next!" The pastor said as he came out and called for the next group.
"That's us." Amy confirmed as they walked into the room.
"Take a seat." Shaun said to his parents as they sat down on the seats.
"We are gathered here today to marry Shaun and Amy." The pastor said as he was looking at his notes. Shaun and Amy then looked at each other as they smiled. Shaun had uncontrollable nerves as he didn't know what to say or do.
"It's okay." Amy said as they held hands and looked at each other. The pastor went on and on and said all the normal things that he needed to say.
"Do you Shaun, take Amy to be your lawful wedded wife?" Shaun nodded his head as he was so happy. "Do you Amy, take Shaun to be your lawful wedded husband." Amy smiled as she said,
"Yes!"
"Well you may now kiss the bride." The pastor said as they embraced each other and snogged for two whole minutes.
"Okay that's enough." Shaun's father said as they stopped kissing.
"I'm so happy." Amy said.
"Well you are going to be an amazing daughter in law." Shaun's mother said as the four of them smiled.

"We have a little surprise for you two." Shaun's dad said as he pulled something out his pocket.
"Here." He said as he gave him the car keys. Shaun looked amazed as she couldn't believe it.
"Is this what I think it is?"
"Go outside and see it."
"Oh wow." Shaun said as Amy was so cheerful she ran outside as she saw the car outside.
"SHAUN!" She screamed as she was joyful. She got into the car as Shaun followed behind her.
"We are going to be so happy together." Amy said as Shaun started up the car.
"I love you!" They both said in sync as they laughed. The car's engine was rumbling as Shaun's parents looked at them drive off into the distance as they started their new life together.

Fin

George's life was boring until one day he meets Amy and falls in love. Follow George as his life changes in an instance as one thing goes to another. From running his sweet shop to going to prison, discover how George survives in this crazy life. Is Amy really the person she says she is as there is a massive secret set to drive George and Amy apart. Is George really the one for Amy or is there someone else waiting in the wings? Find out in this story that has all the dramas and twists and turns.